Christmas in Crickley Creek

Christmas in Crickley Creek

A Crickley Creek Romance

Laurie Beach

TULE
PUBLISHING

Dedication

For my grandparents,
and in loving memory of my little brother, Chris Lokken.

Chapter One

EMMA SHEA HAD a bag ready to go. She'd packed her most expensive items: her Prada oversized sunglasses, all four Louis Vuitton purses, and her collection of Chanel and Tory Burch dresses. What would happen to her three-carat wedding ring? Well, tradition dictated that, since she went through with the marriage, she'd get to keep it. She sat beneath the Christmas lights on the piazza. He'd paid five hundred dollars to have them strung. She chose the lights, of course, and handled the details of the project. Which is why she chose the color red. She hated red at all other times of year except for Christmas, when it suddenly became her preferred accent color.

It might have something to do with the fact that her husband, Trent Broadway, preferred white lights that hung like icicles. With him out of town all the time and Christmas lights nothing less than a requirement for the historic homes in downtown Beaufort, she found a way to sneakily piss him off. She'd been raised in the South, so she was good at inserting the knife and twisting it while looking as sweet and innocent as a kitten.

Who me? I would never. I just adore the color red. I had no idea my husband did not. What has gotten into that man?

The glowing lights on their symmetrical Classic Revival home were as screaming loud and as inappropriate as the red-light district in that Amsterdam place overseas somewhere. The lights made her feel better, like she'd vandalized perfection. They were her version of graffiti.

Emma sat twirling her fingers in her auburn hair. Auburn, because she refused to call it red. She'd found comfort in the soft, strong strands of her own wavy hair as long as she could remember. In many of her childhood photos, her fingers held a pinch of it as she rubbed the strands together, over and over. She spread the soft tresses across her lips—she needed comfort now.

It was just a few months past the one-year anniversary of her wedding, and the media had spilled her secret. LIVE5NEWS began the broadcast that afternoon with pictures of her in her couture wedding gown hugging her mother-in-law. They showed her kissing Trent at the altar and ended with several pictures of her working at the coffee shop, looking a little too happy and standing a little too close to Scruggs Willingham III. What had Emma Shea Broadway been doing in Crickley Creek only weeks before her wedding? Why was she working? And more importantly, who was the guy?

It was big news because her now-husband had plans to run for governor of South Carolina. At thirty, he'd be the youngest governor by far, beating out Nikki Haley by twelve years. Add to that the fact that Emma Shea, formerly Abernathy, was the Beaufort version of Paris Hilton—only rather than hotels, her grandparents, and now her parents, owned all of the Burger Kings and Zaxby's in ten counties, and the pairing made for great ratings. One of the many downsides of kissing up to the press in order to get them to cover boring speeches and charity events was that they were teed up and ready to go as soon as they caught a whiff of scandal. Had Emma Shea Broadway been living a double life? The public wanted to know.

Emma Shea heard the door of the carriage house open and Trent's new black Porsche pull in. She took a deep breath and tugged her fingers from her hair. Maybe putting up the red lights hadn't been such a great idea.

Trent went straight to the piazza, as Emma knew he would. She sat there often, for the fresh air, for the comforting sounds of the frogs, crickets, and cicadas, and to get away from his whirlwind of energy, his constant phone conversations, and his too-loud laugh. She heard the squeak of the screen door and then the slam as he let it go.

A few seconds later, he stood tall and defined in his Dior suit and yellow bow tie, his face void of emotion except for the slight flare of his nostrils. His slicked-back hair made him look exactly like her daddy. The nighttime sounds seemed to grow louder, and she was afraid that if he said something, she wouldn't hear him. But his words were as clear as the sky on the day they were married.

"I'm done."

"I know," she said, dropping her eyes to her hands in her lap.

"You need to leave." His tone sounded like he was telling a waiter there was a fly in his water. He didn't even give her the satisfaction of anger—that would have meant he cared.

"I know," she said again, motioning to the suitcase next to her chair. She was the one in the wrong, so it was clear that she must be the one to give up her comfortable home on the edge of the Beaufort River.

"I'll have my lawyers draw up the papers."

"I'll just take my car," she stood, surprised at how wobbly she felt.

"Fine." He took two steps backward.

It was strange how she felt compelled to hug him. Despite a year of acting happily married to the world while awkwardly ignoring each other in private, it seemed the right thing to do. Finally, they'd given in to the misery and gotten to goodbye. It felt like the one true thing they'd accomplished together. And, somehow, that seemed worthy of a hug. But the same thing that held her back from embracing their marriage held her back from the hug as well. It was her. If she thought she was supposed to hug him, she'd hug him. But it wasn't clear what propriety, or her heart, called for in that instance. She stood in front of him wondering what to do, at battle with herself. So she did nothing.

He turned around and walked inside, letting the screen door slam again.

"Goodbye, Trent," she whispered. He hadn't always been awful. There was a time when they'd been good friends, when they'd laughed and planned for their future and marched into events like royalty, knowing they were the couple that everyone envied. From the silk-lined pocket of her black pants, she pulled out a key. On one side of the degrading yellow plastic key ring was an advertisement for a savings and loan, and on the other side was an address: 19 Blue Ghost Lane, Crickley Creek.

Of all the places. It probably wasn't smart to go back to Crickley Creek when the press was swarming like locusts. But aside from crashing at a friend's house or finding a hotel, it was her only option. She put the key back in her pocket and dragged her suitcase down the steps—*thunk, thunk, thunk*—to her car.

The headlights of her Mercedes SUV shone bright on the street ahead, and she found herself smiling at the familiar route back to the tiny town. Trent Broadway didn't feel real, like the past year of her life was a badly written chapter she'd just torn from the book and thrown into the trash. She felt nothing, except for a healthy dose of guilt about feeling nothing. She should probably be heartbroken or embarrassed or at the very least, filled up with shame and regret. But the one thing she knew for sure was that she wasn't any of those. Not one bit.

Her GPS took her through downtown Crickley Creek, past Tea and Tennyson. She slowed down to look inside, but it was dark. Even the upstairs window where her co-worker, Krista, used to live seemed completely uninhabited. What had she expected? That it would be bright and happy and filled with people drinking coffee and reading books at nine o'clock on a Friday night? They closed at four, for God's sake.

She exited the red-brick downtown as quickly as she arrived, heading toward the peninsula on the outskirts of town, right before Katu Island. There were five short streets there with the creek and the marsh on the left and the Atlantic on the right. Her GPS led her to the street on the far right, and she drove slowly along the beach past a line of old homes. She knew enough about the sea islands to identify the historic ones—some were probably built back when the plantation owners would escape the summertime heat by heading to their homes on the ocean. She counted the numbers on the mailboxes until she landed on sad little number nineteen. It was the most overgrown plot of land, with a dilapidated house painted mossy green sitting right up against the street. She couldn't even see the front door for the big crepe myrtle badly in need of a trim and the masses of ferns and elephant ears. She pulled onto the short gravel driveway and put the car in Park. There was only an open carport, no garage, which meant her new Mercedes would be subject to the ravages of salty air. Clearly, she wouldn't be staying in the falling-apart mystery house long.

The fact that the house even existed was strange. Her mother had stopped by after the salacious news first hit and handed her daughter the key. "Stay here," she said. "It's mine." She patted her daughter's hand and shot her a look of sympathy before dashing back to her car. "Do not tell your father where you are." That was it.

Emma shouldn't have been surprised. There were so many secrets in her family, it was no wonder she'd spent her entire life having no idea her mother owned an ancient beach house in Crickley Creek.

The neighborhood was quiet, and the steady swoosh of waves hit nearby like the ocean knew she'd arrived and was trying to move up the beach to greet her. She used her cell phone flashlight to illuminate the way as she stepped carefully over weeds in between the flagstone leading to the front door. Just as she pulled out the key, she saw something move on her left. On the rim of a bright red pot filled with the remnants of a dead plant was a fuzzy black caterpillar, a woolly bear. Emma knew what that meant: the blacker the woolly bear, the longer and snowier winter would be. Of course, South Carolina rarely saw snow, especially in the Lowcountry, so it surely meant nothing.

She put the key in the lock. It worked.

Chapter Two

THE DOOR CREAKED like the hinges were made before the Civil War, and the stale air inside smelled like firewood and mouse droppings. She aimed her cell phone flashlight toward the nearest wall to find a light switch. When she finally found it, she flipped it up, but nothing happened.

"Dang it," she said. Hopefully, it was just that particular switch. The wood floor creaked as she stepped farther in, closing the door behind her. It was colder inside the house than it was outside. Despite the seventy-degree day, it was nearing fifty now. She shivered. Straight ahead was a narrow wooden staircase with a small hallway to the left and a larger hallway to the right. She shined her light down the wider space. It was far too creepy to shine the light all around, so she moved quickly toward the rear windows and ended up in a kitchen.

Here, she found another yellowing light switch. She flipped it up and down. Nothing happened. She would have chucked her phone at the wall in frustration if she thought she could find it again. It was like all of her bad choices were coming back to bite her all at once: Lying to Scruggs. Marrying Trent. Trusting her mother to help her. What were her options? Sleep in her car? Drive to a cheap motel somewhere? She might be an heiress, but her parents made damn sure she didn't have access to her trust fund until she was thirty, and that was in another four years.

From beyond the kitchen and past the back porch, the moon reflected off the deep Atlantic waters. Not only was it warmer outside, it was considerably brighter, too. She took a pinch of her hair and rubbed the strands together as she made her way to the porch. The tide was in and the ocean was so loud it drowned out her thoughts, leaving only a desperate mantra, *you're okay. You're going to be okay.*

She stepped back inside. She'd just had the guts to leave her husband, she could certainly stay one night in a house with no electricity. All she needed to do was find a bed. Her stomach reminded her that she hadn't eaten dinner. Thankfully, there was enough natural light to root around a bit. The refrigerator was empty except for a water filtration pitcher, Duke's mayonnaise, and a bottle of ketchup. She opened cupboard doors until she found canned soups and crackers. Bean and bacon soup sounded like an option, and it was only a month expired, so she looked around for a saucepan. Ugh. It wasn't worth the effort. She put the can back on the shelf. It was past nine, anyway. According to her intermittent fasting diet, she shouldn't eat past six P.M.

"It's okay to feel hungry," she told herself. "This is what

you have to do to stay a size two." Gaining weight now, while the eyes of the community were all focused on her, would be a disaster. Maybe she would not only skip breakfast tomorrow, she would skip lunch, too.

With no electricity, she'd have to conserve the battery on her phone and quickly find a bed, so she made her way back to the front and took the stairs, deciding the narrow hallway on the left was far too creepy. Each stair had its own creak and groan, and by the time she made it to the landing at the top, she felt like she'd just had a conversation. The only direction to turn was to the right, where her own reflection in a full-length mirror scared the wits out of her. She had to stop for a moment so her heart rate could slow down, and still it took some gumption and a deep breath to keep moving forward.

She tiptoed past the mirrored alcove into an open door where a four-poster bed stood regal in the middle of a small room. It was still freezing upstairs, but the bright white covers looked fluffy and warm. To her left was a giant picture window facing the ocean. She was drawn to it like a bug to a light. The most talented artist of all had created a soft sandy entrance leading to a watery world full of mystery and beauty and promise. She sighed at the view, one anxiety-filled breath escaping, with many more to go.

To her left was a lemon-yellow tiled bathroom with verbena soap at the sink and fluffy white towels hanging by the shower. She turned on the faucet and was relieved that a strong stream of water came out. "Okay," she told herself. "I can do this." Without bothering to retrieve her luggage from the car or take off her clothes, she washed her face, kicked off her shoes, and climbed underneath the covers. She prayed the linens were clean and made an effort not to pull the comforter up against her face. Her mother certainly wouldn't give her a key to a place where someone was currently living, right? Judging from the dust, the weeds, and the lack of electricity, not a soul had been here for a long while. She turned over, pressed her face into the pillow, and shimmied down until the duvet completely covered the back of her head.

It was after seven when the sun's rays beat their warm morning wake-up through the wavy-glassed upstairs windows. Emma Shea opened her eyes, remembering immediately where she was—a beach house that somehow her mother had a key for. Now that she could see clearly, she looked around the wallpapered room. It was straight out of some era long ago, with ladies in puffy pink dresses tending to little white sheep on a yellow background dotted with green palm trees, beige fences, and pink flowers. The carpet was shag and yellow, except for the most traveled areas, which were a grayish brown. Clearly, whoever owned the home hadn't remodeled it since, like, 1960. How embarrassing for whoever lived here. Didn't they take any pride in appearances?

Grateful that the toilet flushed, she finger-combed her

long hair and swished her mouth with water. Then she checked herself in the full-length alcove mirror before taking the steep, narrow stairs to the bottom floor, hoping there was a modern coffeemaker in the kitchen before remembering she had no electricity. The only place in Crickley Creek for a good cup of coffee was Tea and Tennyson, but there was no way she was going there without full makeup and a fresh outfit. Even though her old boyfriend, Scruggs, surely no longer worked there, she still needed to look her best. Scruggs had been set to graduate college with a master's degree in architecture this past spring, so by now his career would be underway and he would no longer be making coffee drinks.

He was taking the media heat now just as sure as she was, and he was probably furious. Not only had she left him without an explanation, she'd now brought his integrity into question. Shame flooded her. He was suddenly the "other" man, when the truth was, he'd never known she was engaged to begin with.

She walked past the front room and glanced out the windows. Her car was still there, untouched, but with a layer of wetness from the early morning fog. As her eyes traveled to her neighbor's house, she noticed a hunched old man carefully unfolding an American flag and attaching it to a pole in his front yard. It was early December; it couldn't be Veteran's Day. She watched as he pulleyed the flag to the top. Something about the sight sent her emotions running as high as the flag, and when the man saluted it, disappointment burned in her chest as hot as cannon fire. She was living in a country that was supposed to be filled with dreams and hopes and opportunity, but the life she thought she wanted—the life that was expected of her—was over. She had no idea what to do next.

Hoping her father was out golfing this Saturday morning, she texted her mother.

"Does this place have electricity? Who lives here? Will they be coming home?"

Clarissa Abernathy's name popped onto her phone screen immediately. *"No one is coming. Salt gets in the light switches. Move them up and down to clear it out."*

"Since when have you owned a beach house?" Emma responded.

"It belonged to your great-great-grandmother, Frances Mackey," she answered.

The crazy one? Emma had heard about Crazy Frannie her whole life. The woman was a bootlegger during Prohibition. She'd found a way to survive after her husband died, even though it was entirely inappropriate. Emma looked around the home with fresh eyes—the art deco stained glass on the front door, the gold palm-leafed fireplace screens, the black-and-white floor in the kitchen with green tiled counters. Everything about the house was female, with no male influence to be seen. No dark-brown recliners or cigar boxes, only light-gold velvet club chairs and brightly colored vases and urns on every surface. Even the mahogany woodwork was accented with vibrant paintings.

Emma started to put it all together. *"So you inherited it from your mama?"*

The answer was immediate. *"Got to go. Your daddy's on his way home."*

Emma knew her mother would be deleting the conversation in case Daddy decided to take a look at her phone. He was a man who expected his one-and-only daughter to grow up worthy of his investment in her. She was like one of his mutual funds—if she didn't perform well, she would be dumped. And, considering he wouldn't allow her back into her former home, it was as clear as Crazy Frannie's crystal foyer chandelier that Emma was no longer considered worthy of the Abernathy name. And if her mother didn't watch her step, she'd be dropped, too.

Emma was starving, and canned soup for breakfast did not sound appealing. Neither did a cup of coffee made from an expired bag of coffee grounds. It probably wouldn't be smart to go into Tea and Tennyson since that was the scene of her crime with Scruggs, so her new plan was to drag in her suitcase, gussy herself up, and head to the local Piggly Wiggly for groceries. She flipped the light switch in the hallway up and down at least ten times before one large white overhead light flickered and glowed. "I guess you're letting me know up front how it's gonna be, huh?" she said out loud to the house before going through and wiggling every light switch in the place and getting a tour of the house while she was at it.

The narrow hallway she'd seen to the left of the stairs led to a guest bedroom. It was small, but the tall iron bed was beautifully made and stationed next to a fireplace. On the exterior wall to her left was a door leading to a sleeping porch with a swing wide enough to take a nap on. It began to occur to her that not only did the house not have heat, it didn't have air-conditioning, either. Everything was set up to find comfort in other ways. Ways she'd never had to deal with before—like lighting a fire or sleeping outside where she'd be lucky to get a breeze. No wonder the place smelled like firewood.

When the front door creaked at her, she told it to hush and stepped into the chilly morning air. There, on a small plant table next to one of the red pots, was an apple. She picked it up. It was plump and red and perfectly apple-shaped without a bruise or a scratch on it. She was certain it hadn't been there the night before. Glancing around, not one person was outside on Blue Ghost Lane, and there didn't appear to be an apple on anyone else's front stoop. Had the old man left it for her? She frowned at the piece of fruit.

"Where did you come from?" Bringing it with her to the car, she placed it on the console, pulled out her suitcase, then came back to it. The fact was, she was starving. She looked around at the empty street again thinking to herself, *you know you're lower than low when you eat something you found outside.*

What did she have to lose? Juice dribbled down her chin when she took a bite. It was the sweetest, most perfect piece of fruit she'd ever tasted.

Chapter Three

"WELL, I'LL BE danged, if it ain't our long-lost Emma Smith. Or should I say Broadway? Or Abernathy? I just can't keep it all straight anymore." Birdalee Mudge-Crane wore a fuzzy red sweater with huge green jingle bells hanging off a bow on the front. She had a Cornish game hen in each hand when Emma came up on her in the Piggly Wiggly.

Emma was acutely aware that she was in the grocery store wearing a Chanel dress and high-heeled Jimmy Choos when the rest of the world was in sweatpants. When she'd packed to leave so quickly, she hadn't been in her right mind and couldn't bear to leave behind her best outfits. Now she had not one stitch of casual wear. None of her outfits was appropriate for an average day in Crickley Creek. And of all the people to run into, it had to be Birdalee Mudge-Crane? The woman had a mouth bigger than both the Carolinas put together and absolutely no tact. Emma attempted to scoot past her to the fresh chicken tenderloins.

Birdie put the hens in her cart and yelled toward Emma's back, "You know, you're not the only one getting media attention these days."

Emma turned around, assuming Birdie was talking about their resident online influencer, Krista Hassell. She'd single-handedly brought tourism to Crickley Creek with her outdoor adventure videos and veterans charity. Emma liked her. They'd worked together at Tea and Tennyson back before Emma's life went to hell in a handbasket.

"Oh, for heaven's sake, no. Not Krista." Birdie put a hand on her meaty hip. "Have you not been following my YouTube channel? I call it What's in the Flask? Also known as Birdalee's School of Manners. Look it up. Tonight I am teaching my fans how to properly eat a quail." She glanced toward the game hens in her cart. "No one will know."

"Sounds great," Emma said, turning to go again. "I'll be sure to watch it."

"Oh no you don't." Birdie shoved her cart in front of Emma, nearly running over her foot in the process. "There is no such thing as coincidences, so I know for a fact that you are standing here in front of me for a reason. The whole town is talking about you and my most favorite architect on the whole entire earth, Master Scruggs Willingham the Third." She said his name as if it were an announcement.

Emma couldn't help but bite. "Master?"

"Well, he's got his master's degree. It should be a thing. Why should doctors have all the fun?" Suddenly, Birdie's frenetic motion and subsequent *jingle-jangle* halted like a thought just hit her over the head. "What did you say you were doing here in the Crickley Creek Piggly Wiggly?"

Emma hadn't said, and didn't plan to.

Birdie looked brazenly into Emma's basket. "Toilet paper, coffee, milk, All-Bran. You are planning to sit on the pot somewhere. Where are you staying and why are you back?"

Emma's face felt hot. The woman was completely without couth. "Those are excellent questions, and I would love to tell you." She moved Birdie's cart to the side, clearing her way. "But I don't know."

"For pity's sake, don't try to tell me you don't know where you're staying. Hand to God, I won't tell anyone."

As if. Birdie was the Paul Revere of Crickley Creek. "I am not ready to talk about it yet."

"Well then. When you are ready, come back to Tea and Tennyson and tell us all about it. As you know, I am there every weekday by eight for my breakfast." She turned her cart back toward the tiny hen section of the meat department. "I'll see you on Monday."

"I—" Emma began.

Birdie used her forefinger and thumb in a clamping motion and grunted at the same time—the universal sign to shut up. So Emma did. But no matter what Birdie proclaimed, there was no way she would go back to Tea and Tennyson. She wasn't ready. Yet.

In the light of day, Crazy Frannie's house was more of a deep Christmas green than mossy. Add to that the red pots by the front door and it looked like it had been dropped onto a South Carolina beach from some little village in the North Pole. A plastic Santa sleigh with reindeer led by Rudolph would suit the pitched roof perfectly. For the smallest second, she felt the old excitement about Christmas that she'd felt as a kid. But that left quickly. She was alone. At least for the time being.

She had hope that her father would soften in time for her to come home for the holiday. He'd never been the family-first type, but maybe he'd miss her. She looped all five plastic bags over both arms and heaved them from the car. Unlocking the front door was a struggle. Just as it creaked open, a loud meow came from above her head. She stepped back and looked up at a scruffy orange cat, staring angrily down at her from the roof. "Well, hello there," she said.

The cat didn't flinch. It was like he was staking a claim on the home and making it clear she was not welcome.

"Nice to meet you, too," she said before entering the dusty house and kicking the creaky door shut behind her.

She was hungry again. The apple had been the perfect breakfast, but she was desperate for coffee and a biscuit. If Trent had seen her putting a frozen biscuit into the oven, he would have been appalled. Biscuits were supposed to be made from scratch, and she was the housewife who was supposed to do it. Additionally, the extra effort for a perfect flaky biscuit was simply to be done and not mentioned or complained about.

It was the least of his many expectations.

She clunked two white hockey pucks onto a tray and slid them into the oven. By the time they were golden brown, her coffee was ready. She found a black tray on top of the refrigerator and read the painted words before using it to carry her biscuit, coffee, dish of butter, knife, and muscadine jelly onto the back porch. HUNNUH MUS TEK CYEAR A DE ROOT FAH HEAL DE TREE. She knew it was in the Gullah language but had no idea what it meant.

The day was sunny and she didn't even need a sweater to sit outside. After setting the tray on the old wicker coffee table, she kicked off the slippers she'd found in the closet and chose the rocking chair closest to the back door. It was Charleston green, which looked like black, but she knew better. She looked up—the ceiling was haint blue, just as it should be.

She rocked for a while, making sure she didn't hit the wall behind her. It was covered in real shells like they were wallpaper. She didn't miss Trent. She didn't even miss her mother. But she missed having her people. She missed having somewhere to be, someone to look after her. Someone to talk to. She had friends in Beaufort, of course, but they were the kind that celebrated with you when things were good and disappeared when you did something embarrassing. Did anyone truly miss her? Of course, she'd only been gone one day, so it might be too soon to tell.

She pulled up the Louis Vuitton website and scrolled through the purses. Imagining herself with a big new one made her feel better. People would know she wasn't just some nobody if she had a purse like that. They'd know how on-trend and relevant she was. They'd want to be like her. She slammed her phone down on the coffee table. She didn't want friends who only liked her for her purse.

But she still wanted the camel-colored Louis Vuitton Cluny bag. Badly.

A loud, guttural *meow* made her jump. "Ya danged cat!" This time he glared at her from the long wooden walkway leading from the back porch down to the beach. "Where'd you come from, and why are you yelling at me?"

He answered with a hiss.

"Well, I don't like you either." She took a belligerent bite of her biscuit. "And this is not your house—it is my mother's."

It was just like Crickley Creek to have low-class, no-manners cats. Whereas her hometown of Beaufort was like a miniature Charleston, complete with blue bloods and old society rules, this place was the strangest combination of rich Southern history and a down-home sort of humility. Beaufort and Charleston did not partake in humility. And it felt like Crickley Creek was on a mission to humble her. Or maybe it was to humiliate her. Both seemed a version of the same word. Birdie in the grocery store was a prime example—she may be married to a pastor, but her mission was more to spread gossip than to save souls. It probably took under ten minutes for the entire town to know that Emma was back. And how strange that she even had a connection here, especially considering her mother had one, too.

Before she'd briefly escaped Beaufort by driving aimlessly around the South Carolina Lowcountry two years ago, she'd never heard of Crickley Creek. Led only by instinct and the luxury of extra time, she stopped in the little downtown business district to use the restroom and get a refreshment. Never did she expect that when she walked into the black-and-white store filled with books and knickknacks and warm with the smell of coffee and fresh pastries that her life was about to change.

She made eye contact with a cute boy behind the counter, and he flirted with her by changing the music in the store to "Just the Way You Are" by Bruno Mars. His eyes followed her everywhere, stuck to her like melted marshmallow on a fuzzy sweater, and she ended up applying for and winning an unneeded, unplanned, commute-requiring job as a barista.

That was Crickley Creek's first blow to the only persona she'd ever had—that of a rich, pretty little girl whose family insisted that she be seen and not heard. And when she was seen, she must be perfect. Nothing at Tea and Tennyson required perfection, not the store's owner, Charlotte, not her co-worker Krista, and not the young man behind the counter, who'd named his little dog Waffles and brought her to work every day; the man who gave her flowers made from Legos; the man she'd almost given up everything for: Scruggs

Willingham III.

It was he who she'd abandoned without explanation. He who she'd ghosted when it looked like she might get caught working in a coffee shop in Crickley Creek, of all places. After all, she was already engaged to Trent Broadway, the future governor of the great state of South Carolina—if he won the election. If she didn't go through with the marriage, she would be a disappointment to every family in Beaufort who donated to his campaign, beginning with her own. She didn't have the courage to tell Scruggs what a duplicitous liar she'd been. She hadn't even given him her real name. He knew her as Emma Smith, not Emma Shea Abernathy.

So she'd taken the easy way out and left.

Surely, he knew by now that she was back.

Chapter Four

MONDAY. ANOTHER APPLE, like there had been the day before. She'd checked for the gift of fruit that morning at the crack of dawn, just as the little old man next door hung the flag that he dutifully took down and folded each night. She picked up the apple and waved at him, but he either didn't see her or ignored her. He appeared far too grumpy to leave apples at her door anyway. It couldn't be him. She was going to need to install a front door camera.

"Hi, Mama," she texted from the safety of the small kitchen. *"Are you free this week?"*

It took a while before an answer came through. *"Have you not been keeping up with the news? Your name is mud out here. And best not text me for a while either. Your father and I will be in Florida for the holidays. Pray this is all over when we return."*

It was like getting stabbed in the heart with an airline ticket. The hope Emma Shea had for a Christmas at home had been packed like a snowball and exploded all over the overgrown lawn of the lonely, green house she was now trapped in. And apparently, her good name had, too.

She cut the apple into slices and put it on a cobalt-blue salad plate along with a dollop of peanut butter. She took it to the back porch, strangely hoping the orange cat would be there. She needed someone to talk to, even if that someone was ornery and furry.

By the time she finished the apple, the cat still hadn't shown up. Although it was highly likely he was hiding somewhere stalking her, willing her to leave.

Curiosity got the best of her and she googled Emma Shea Abernathy Broadway. Dozens of headlines popped up: THE LIGHTS WENT OUT ON EMMA SHEA BROADWAY. HIGH CLASS OR NO CLASS? WHERE IS ALLEGED CHEATER EMMA SHEA BROADWAY? She clicked on the article titled BROADWAY STILL LOVES HER.

"He couldn't possibly *still* love me," she said as she skimmed the page. "He never loved me to begin with."

Trent Broadway is using his newfound spotlight to win his wife back. In an unexpected move on Monday, Broadway makes it clear he is willing to work on the marriage with his errant wife, Emma Shea. Photos surfaced last Friday of then-Emma Shea Abernathy cozied up with Scruggs Willingham III at a small-town coffee shop, where it appears they were both employed. The photos were taken only weeks before her marriage to Broadway. Yet Broadway still envisions his wife as the next first lady of South Carolina.

"I am a man of principle and pride myself on hav-

ing the highest level of integrity," Broadway stated. "I made a vow to Emma Shea, and I will work with her to see it through. I gave her my heart years ago, and she still has it."

"Oh, please," she said out loud. She clicked out of the article. "That is the biggest bunch of BS I've ever heard. *Principle and integrity.* More like selfishness and ruthless ambition." She shuddered. Aside from Trent's empty words, what she got from the Google search was that people were looking for her. Trent hadn't so much as called or texted, despite his statement, but the media was on the prowl. It was a good thing she'd stocked up on food, because she might be stuck where she was for a while.

"Cat!" she yelled. "Come here, kitty!" She was in desperate need of companionship. "Please?" There was not one meow or glimpse of orange fur anywhere near. "Fine." She took her plate inside. She'd dug up a pair of old jeans and a floral button-down shirt from the upstairs closet. She put on somebody's wide-brimmed beach hat and her Prada sunglasses and headed toward the beach. It was early on a Monday and the fog was still lifting. There shouldn't be many people out, so it was probably safe to take a walk. She needed an escape and wouldn't go far.

As soon as she reached the end of the long wooden walkway, she saw her neighbor on the beach. The hairline on the back of his semi-bald head looked like it was smiling at her as he sat on an ice chest with the line from his fishing pole cast way out in the water.

She walked up behind him. "Whatcha fishing for?"

He looked at her briefly, the skin around his mouth resembling that of a bulldog. "Hoping for a small shark but only gettin' drum."

"Really? A shark?"

"Ever eat a scallop?" he asked.

"Yes."

"You like it?"

"Yes."

"Well, that's what shark tastes like." He frowned at her. "It's not like I'm hoping for a Great White. The bonnet shark around here are good eatin'."

They gazed out at the ocean together while Emma imagined the old man catching a shark with a head that looked like a bonnet. Should she stay and help him?

"You're Clarissa's daughter," he stated.

"How did you know?" As soon as she said it, she realized it was a dumb question. Her mother owned the house next door, and clearly the man had been around since the invention of the wheel.

"I was twenty years old when I moved in next door to one of your grandmothers—Frances Mackey. She was an old lady at the time, but she still had her wits about her. Frannie was tougher than shoe leather."

"You knew Crazy Frannie?"

His grumpy expression deepened. "Wasn't one crazy

thing about her. That woman had moxie."

He reeled in his line and cast again.

"What if you catch a really big shark?" she asked.

He appeared annoyed by the question. "Then I cut the line."

She was about to wander off when he spoke again. "I got myself a doll of a wife at seventeen, and when I got back from the war, I built her the home of her dreams. That one back there." His lips and hands visibly shook and he pointed behind his shoulder. "Bless her sweet soul. Mary was my best girl."

Emma hadn't expected his sudden softening. Or the emotion. Should she pat him on the shoulder? What did propriety call for? She opted for what she was taught to do when she was uncertain about something—play dumb. "Oh! Is she at home?"

He didn't appear to have heard a word she said, merely tugged on his line, then wiped his eyes with the sleeve of his worn plaid button-down. "Frannie was the first of generations of ladies in your line to stay in that house. It's like she knew all y'all would have the same sort of picking problem."

His grumpiness was back just as fast as he'd wiped away the tears. Was he really coming right out and accusing her family of marrying poorly? The audacity. The distinct lack of manners. She sighed her annoyance loudly.

"I know what that sigh means," he said, "but I have earned the right to speak plainly."

His tone was what she'd been accustomed to her whole life. Just like her daddy, who did not put up with one ounce of sass, he'd put her in her place. "Yes, sir," she said.

"After Frances came Mable Clark, and after Mable came Esther Collins. After Esther came your mother, Clarissa Abernathy. And now here you are, Emma Shea Broadway. See, I knew all of your grandmothers, and I already know your name." With clear enjoyment he added, "And I have to say, you're bringing the talk with you, too. Just like Frannie."

"I'm sure she didn't deserve it."

The old man chuckled. "Oh, she deserved it all right. Have yourself a seat." He motioned toward the sand next to his old blue ice chest.

She really shouldn't sit on the dirty beach sand, and she hadn't brought a towel, but the moment was too intriguing to risk interrupting. So she sat with her knees pulled up to her chin—that way only the smallest portion of her rear was affected.

She could practically hear the twinkle in his eye with every word he spoke.

"Frances was a bootlegger."

"I know," she said. "Word has it she even knew Al Capone."

"The times were called Prohibition. You heard of it?"

Of course she'd heard of it. She nodded.

"Now, I was only seven years old when Prohibition ended, but rumors had it that Frannie was a constant source of hullabaloo around here. There are still some old electrical wires wrapped around the top of the big cinnamon crepe myrtle in the front yard. She lit that tree up with twinkle lights year-round so people would know where to find the booze."

Emma's imagination caught fire—the woman was brazen. She suddenly wanted to know everything about Frances Mackey. Heck, she wanted to *be* Frances Mackey. She could hardly wait to check out the big tree and see if what he said was true.

He reeled in his line, deep in thought. "All of you Mackey women have that gumption in you somewhere. You've just got to find it and aim it in the right direction."

A tall man was walking down the beach toward them. It looked like he held a camera. Emma instantly tensed but didn't want to stop the conversation. She wanted to hear every detail. Keeping her eye on the stranger, she asked, "Did she have a husband?"

"Of course she had a husband. A rotten one, from what I heard. He died young." He cast his line again. "Ah, but Frannie was a looker. She got away with just about anything on account of those long legs of hers. The blonde hair and big blue eyes didn't hurt neither. That dame was older than my mother, but that didn't stop her from walking right out here on this beach in a two-piece swimming suit. She was quite the dish."

The stranger with the camera was approaching. It was definitely a camera, and he held it at the ready. Emma couldn't decide whether to dash inside or stay put and hope the hat and glasses were disguise enough. She quickly tucked her hair underneath the woven fabric, hoping the red strands wouldn't catch his eye. "If that man asks," she said, "we have to give me a different name."

The old man wasn't fazed. "Well, we'll just call you Frannie then."

Chapter Five

THE OLD MAN'S name was Brown Odgers Howell, Brownie for short. When the stranger with the camera came close, Brownie raised a hand and said, "Mornin'." The man said good morning in return. Emma didn't so much as look up. Even though he kept on walking, the close call had set her heart to racing like a lopsided hamster wheel. She probably shouldn't push her luck.

Reluctantly, she left Brownie in his attempt to catch a shark and jogged back to the house. She was past the small dunes and admiring the red camellias growing against the faded white of his wood-paneled house when she noticed he had a rather large apple tree in his yard. Just like that, the early morning apple mystery was solved. Had he done the same for all of the women who stayed in that house? She'd have to remember to thank him next time she saw him.

"Frances Mackey," she said to herself as she walked up the back stairs and opened the back door. How did she have moxie? What even was moxie? She googled it. *Moxie: Force of character, determination, or nerve.* Emma's whole life she'd survived by making sure no one had reason to question her.

She was too nice, if anything. Too quiet. Too passive. But her two times great-grandmother? Well, she was exactly the opposite.

Emma rifled through the boxes in a storage space underneath the stairs, hoping to find a journal or a photo album, anything to learn more about Frannie. Sneezing through the dust she'd stirred up, she found framed pictures of her mother and grandmother, stitched handkerchiefs, completed patchwork quilts, and a pile of tops that had never been basted. She found an old camera, a nurse's hat, and a book of ration coupons with a few still left unused. Most of all there were shells—whelks, coquinas, slipper shells, oyster shells, and dozens more. Her grandmothers, more than one, spent time sewing and collecting and *living* in this house.

Her phone rang. It was Trent. She didn't want to speak with him, but considering the circumstances, she probably should.

"Hello?"

"I know where you are."

"Okay."

"I can track your phone, you know."

"Okay."

"And I called your daddy. He told me your mama has some sort of hovel out there she won't let go of. He knows she gave you the key."

Her stomach lurched. Her mother was going to pay a price for helping her.

"First of all, are you stupid?" he yelled. "You're back in Crickley Creek? Did you go back to that guy? To Scrooge Cunningham or whatever the hell his name is?"

"His name is Scruggs Willingham. And I would love to answer your questions one at a time, Trent." She put on the calmest, most saccharine-sweet voice she could muster. "Number one: no. I am not stupid. Number two: Yes. I like it here. Number three: No. I haven't seen him, and I don't plan to."

"Do you have any idea the kind of damage you are doing to me? I am getting calls all day long from my biggest donors, wanting to know if I'm gonna let you come back."

"I thought any press was good press." It was snarky, but it felt good.

"Are you pretending to be stupid, or have you really lost your mind? Politics is a delicate balance and you are making me look bad."

"I saw the headlines, and I'm pretty sure the only person who looks bad is me."

"Evolution, Emma Shea. The stories are evolving. They always do."

What was that supposed to mean?

"They're saying I knew about your cheating and forced you to marry me anyway."

"Oh." Well, *forced* was a strong word. He had applied pressure, weaving tales of them as a famous power couple and the good she could do as first lady. But back then, she'd thought she was making a good decision. She kept her mouth shut. Years of living with her father had taught her that. Plus, she was just as upset about being portrayed as a victim as she was about being the perpetrator.

She'd married Trent Broadway because she thought she could change him. And, if she was honest with herself, she desperately wanted the historic mansion on the water near downtown Beaufort—the beautiful one the tourists stopped to take photos of. The one with the marble front stairs that were dented and cracked from the Great Skedaddle in 1861. Add to that a handsome, ambitious man like Trent, and she thought she would have everything. Simply by being on his arm, she felt like someone important. It was an extension of being popular in high school—she needed the attention.

Living without adoration was simply impossible to imagine. Would life even be worth living if she wasn't envied? She needed a home where the front steps weren't allowed to be fixed because of their great historical significance. One with a plaque out front. One where others wondered who the lucky people were who got to live there now. And she needed a husband who people craned their necks to look at. He might not be a movie star, but at least he looked like one. She thought her life would be so posh and wonderful that it'd be like living in a gigantic Louis bag.

She heard Trent breathing heavily, a thing he did when he was highly frustrated. "You're going to have to come back," he said.

The sassy part of her wanted to say, *how romantic.* Instead, she said, "I don't think that's a good idea." The truth was, living with him had indeed been like living in a Louis bag—dark, claustrophobic, and sometimes scary. She looked out the window from the kitchen table where she'd spread out the seashells and saw the orange cat walking along the porch railing.

"Emma Shea," he said. "It doesn't matter what either of us thinks right now. We have to do what's right."

What's right for who? "I will certainly give it some thought."

"That is not an answer!"

She heard a bang, like he hit his fist against something. She shuddered. He'd really be mad if he knew there was more to the story. But she would never speak of it as long as she lived.

"Listen up," he said. "You can spend more time out there in your little shack if you want to, but we have to be back together by Christmas. The visuals for the press would be perfect. My mama will do up the Christmas tree in our house. Just make sure you have a nice, classy dress to wear, and not a black one—that would look like you were going to a funeral. Red might make you look like a hussy, so I'm thinking maybe green velvet or something like that."

"I don't have a green velvet dress."

"Well, I left you some spending money in our joint account, so you can go out and get one."

"Left me spending money?"

"Well, I can't risk you taking what's mine, so I moved it."

She shook with anger. "My money was in there, too." She'd been using her nursing degree to fill in at both the hospital and the local hospice organization for the past year. She'd made quite a bit of money, too.

"We'll get it all straightened out when you return. I'll give you a very generous allowance."

Anger boiled so hot and fast, it made her dizzy. She hung up on him.

The cat turned to look at her through the window. What had she done? She'd gone and married someone exactly like her father. The kitchen chair she sat on tipped over when she stood. She left it where it lay and ran outside. She needed some fresh air. The door to the porch slammed shut so hard behind her that the art deco stained glass insert jiggled. She bent over, hands on her knees, trying to get her emotions under control. When she stood, the orange cat was sitting on the railing, staring at her like she was a clown put there solely for his entertainment.

"Stop it," she said.

The cat didn't even blink.

"Stop judging me."

His eyes squinted with what was clearly hatred.

"You are a rotten excuse for a cat," she said.

He stood and stretched like he hadn't a care in the world.

She plopped herself into one of the black rocking chairs and moved back and forth, crunching against the sandy wood, thinking. Then she pulled up her banking app. There was exactly five hundred dollars in her account. Only five hundred? That wouldn't even buy a decent pair of shoes on discount. Anger wasn't a big enough word. She was incensed, hurt, and ready to pull Trent's slicked-back hair out by the roots. He should have no say in how much of *her* money she spent.

She was pissed, and she didn't care who knew it.

Pulling up Twitter, she considered writing about what a terrible husband he was in 280 characters or less. That would feel like sweet revenge. Then it occurred to her—if the press was positioning Trent as the bad guy, maybe it was safe for her to venture out of the house. Wouldn't the press be looking for him to make a wrong move? Wouldn't they be much more interested in taking photos of the villain than the victim? Maybe she could risk going to Tea and Tennyson. She'd been happier there than any other place in the world. And even if the press tracked her down, getting coffee was not a crime. Even if it was in Crickley Creek. Why was she letting him, the media, or other people's stupid opinions keep her away? Dammit, she was going to have moxie, too. Plus, Scruggs no longer worked there.

As quickly as she'd sat, she jumped back up. She still had Krista's and Charlotte's phone numbers. She would text them and see if they would meet her there in the morning.

Chapter Six

ASIDE FROM VARIOUS sizes of Christmas trees and presents in the windows, big gold bows on every bookshelf, and a table filled with boxed chocolates and Christmas books, Tea and Tennyson hadn't changed a bit. The black-and-white floors with the little tile path that led to the back patio, the clear acrylic chairs, bookshelves on every wall and modern crystal chandeliers in the center—there was nothing else like it anywhere she'd ever been. The chalkboard menu was still behind the counter, with Birdie's concoction in the number one spot and the only thing written in purple. Maybe for old times' sake, Emma would order the Early Birdie Special—a truckload of caffeine, sugar, and chocolate might make the social gathering easier.

Her heart pounded like a hammer as she looked around for Charlotte or Krista.

"Well, if it ain't our errant debutant." Birdie appeared out of nowhere, like she'd flown down from some rafter and landed smack in front of Emma. "We had us a date on Monday, remember? Now I know your mother did not raise you without manners."

I never agreed to that meeting. "Yes, ma'am. I apologize." Saying the words made her stomach burn.

"Did we just hear Emma?" Krista came running down from the back stairs that led to the loft where she used to live. She was even more beautiful, if that were possible. Still tanned in the middle of winter, with her long blond hair as straight and shiny as silk, she practically glowed with happiness. "Come here, you. It's been too long." She grabbed Emma into a hug.

Following slowly behind her was a very pregnant Charlotte Rushton. "Is our girl back in town? Hi, honey." She took her turn hugging Emma before waddling her way to a table in the corner while answering all of Emma's baby questions. They were due on New Year's Eve, they didn't know the gender, and yes, Will was more excited than a hunting dog with a duck about being a daddy.

Birdie, despite the lack of invitation, came with them.

"You've been going through it, haven't you?" Despite having lived in Crickley Creek for years, Charlotte still sounded like a Californian. There was no hint of an accent.

"Yes, but let's talk about you," Emma said. "How are you feeling?"

"Oh, I'm fine," Charlotte said.

"Any names picked out?"

"We're thinking about naming her Anna Grace after my mother if it's a girl, but we don't have a boy's name picked out yet."

"I keep telling her she should name him Ashby," Birdie interjected. "My husband would be so thrilled, and you know we won't be having any babies at our age. Our insides are like a fruit salad left outside to dry."

Charlotte smiled patiently. "We love Ashby, of course. But we're leaning toward a family name." They all pulled out a chair and sat.

"*Chosen* family, my dear. Ever heard of it?" Birdie noisily dumped her enormous purse on the ground, then scooted in her chair. "Your mother chose me as her best friend back in pre-school, and that means you've got me whether you want me or not." She turned her eyes as far away from Charlotte as they'd go without moving her whole head—a sure sign she was annoyed.

"Do you have a place out here?" Krista asked Emma. "Cause Johnny and I've got some empty buildings on the property if you need somewhere to lay your head."

"Thank you, but apparently, my mother owns a beach house down the street." Emma shrugged.

"You have got to be kidding me," Birdie said, her lips forming a small *O* at the fact that there was something she didn't know about Crickley Creek "Where is it?"

"On the peninsula out by the marina. There are like thirty houses out there."

She could almost hear the computer in Birdie's head clicking. "Of course I know that place. Old, old homes out there. Some of them date back to the mid-1800s." Her eyes grew wide. "Is the home…historic?"

"If you consider the 1920s historic. I believe hers is one of the newer homes."

"Whew." Birdie exhaled loudly. "We're safe to tell Virginia then."

Charlotte and Krista both rolled their eyes.

"Why would she care?" Emma asked.

"I do not have the patience to get into it. But her home in Charleston is south of Broad, of course. That sort of thing matters to her."

Why on earth would a fifty-something-year-old woman have any feeling one way or another about her mother's inherited home? But Emma's wonderment was short-lived. A familiar voice coming from upstairs captured every bit of her attention. It was like her heart was a clock that seized and ground to a stop the minute she heard his voice.

She turned in time to see Scruggs take the last step into the room. He didn't look like a college student anymore. He looked like a man. He still wore his signature khakis and wrinkled button-down shirt, but he'd shaved the beard that was just beginning to sprout the last time she saw him. His brown hair was still a backward mullet—longish in the front but military short in the back. He was taller, but he flipped his bangs to the right just like he always had.

Most of all, his blue eyes still arrested her. She thought she might pass out from the thrill of seeing him. Charlotte and Krista must not have told him she was coming, because when his eyes landed on her, a flash of something intense hit his face. Recognition, mixed with what? She held her breath. He had every reason to be angry with her, to hate her. But was it possible that the shock she saw spread over his face was desire? He stopped talking and walking at the same time. It was like the whole store fell still once their eyes met.

But he recovered quickly. He resumed speaking to the man beside him and moved past her as if she weren't there.

So, that was how it was going to be.

"Screwtape!" Birdie yelled, purposefully butchering his name. "What has gotten into you? That was rude."

"Birdie!" Emma shushed her. "It's okay. I deserve it."

Scruggs didn't even turn. He just walked out the front door.

"Of course you deserve it, we all know that," Birdie said. "But a gentleman is never supposed to act ignorant. He is supposed to face things head-on."

"I'm so sorry," Charlotte said. "I didn't think to tell you he was here. I'm turning the upstairs into a day spa. He's my architect."

What a great idea. Charlotte was on to something big. Crickley Creek was in desperate need of a spa, and Scruggs was the perfect, most creative person to design it.

"Mama!" Krista yelled across the store as they all sat themselves. "Can you make us some peppermint mochas?"

Junie was lounging behind the counter since no customers were near. She jumped up, pulling her too-short T-shirt down beneath her apron. "Y'all should have our new sweet tea floats," she said. "They ain't Christmas-y, but it ain't cold outside neither. They come straight from that Southern Market in Beaufort, you know."

The other women nodded at Krista. "We'll have the lemon sorbet in our floats. Thanks, Mama."

"How long are you staying?" Charlotte asked Emma.

"I would love to tell you, but I have no idea," she said.

"Listen, I know people are all a-titter about your marriage right now, but just like any other gossip, it will pass," Birdie said. "I mean, I've seen your Mr. Trent Fancypants Broadway on the television, and the stupidity is laying right on his face. You didn't do anything to his career that he wasn't about to do himself."

Charlotte shot Birdie a look while Krista reached out and patted Emma's hand. "This will all blow over," she said.

"None of this is a big deal," Birdie said. "And I'm sure Charlotte will give you your old job back if you need it."

Her old job would barely pay the insurance on her Mercedes.

Charlotte smiled. "Of course."

The jingle bells on the front door jangled, but they did that all day long, and they'd all learned to ignore it. It wasn't until she saw Charlotte's eyes widen that Emma turned to look. Scruggs was back, and from the pace of his walk, he had no intention of remaining ignorant. He marched straight to their table, his face redder than the apple she'd had for breakfast.

"I need to talk to you." He spoke directly at Emma, ignoring everyone else at the table.

"Well, hello to you, too," Birdie said.

"Stick a cork in it, Turd-a-lee," he said. Birdie was his childhood neighbor and practically his aunt. They lived to annoy each other.

"Of course," Emma answered, scooting her chair backward and standing. She hoped no one noticed she was shaking. "Will y'all excuse me, please?"

"Go," Charlotte said while Krista smiled encouragingly. Birdie shooed them away with her hand.

Emma followed Scruggs as he led her out the back door to the patio. She'd never been on that patio without his dog running up to greet her. Waffles had practically been the store mascot the entire time they worked there together. The dog's absence made her sad for how things had changed. "Is Waffles okay?" she asked.

Scruggs didn't answer. He chose a table directly underneath the oak tree and pulled out a chair for himself. When they were a couple, he'd always pull out the chair for her first. He sat. "She's fine."

Tears welled hot, but they were from more than the fact that she was sitting here with Scruggs than that the dog was okay. Although she was relieved to hear the little creature was still alive, she'd forgotten how attracted she was to Scruggs. How simply being near him gave her a warm, tingly rush.

"Why?" Scruggs asked, his mouth in a straight line.

"I'm so sorry."

"There is no sorry here, okay? It is too late for sorry. You were my girlfriend, Emma. I—" He stopped. "Then you up and leave, and next thing I know you're married? What in the hell?"

"I know." She wiped at her tears, knowing they only made things worse. She didn't deserve to act like a victim.

"Why would anyone do something so God-danged mean?"

"That's a really good question," she said.

He shook his head as if the pent-up frustration he'd been holding on to was threatening to bust out of his face.

"I don't have an answer that is good enough," she said.

"Try."

Goodness knows she'd tried to make sense of it herself. "I guess I wanted that life, and I wanted to please my parents, and I thought it was my only chance."

"What kind of life are you talking about? Being married to some slickster? Is that what you wanted?"

"I thought it was the life I was supposed to have."

"So why aren't you living it, then? Because someone snitched to the press?"

"Yes, and I'm so sorry."

"So, if my name wasn't in every news outlet this side of the Mississippi right now, you'd still be with him."

"Well—" She didn't know how to answer the question.

"It's more complicated than that."

His face turned from red to pale and he shook his head and looked away.

"You're the kind of guy who makes flowers out of Legos," she began.

"What in the hell is that supposed to mean?"

"Trent would have someone else buy me flowers. He didn't make time for me. He ignored me. He bossed me around. I don't know. It's just that marrying him felt comfortable—like what I was used to at home."

Scruggs shook his head, this time like he was trying to rattle out the pain. "So, what you're saying is that I loved you too much? I was too good of a boyfriend?"

"I don't know." She wondered if she should say what she was thinking, but it came out of her mouth before she realized she'd decided. "I mean, he wasn't always horrible. But I never stopped missing you. I knew I'd made a mistake right away."

He pointed his finger at her, the color instantly back in his face. "Don't ever say that again. I have a girlfriend now."

He stood quickly, like she'd pressed a hidden eject button. "Okay," she said.

"I can't believe a word that comes out of your mouth, Emma. And because of you, my mama is embarrassed to show her face around town. She didn't raise me to be anybody's *other* man. This is affecting my family and my work now. I couldn't even bid on a job yesterday because people recognized my name. They think I have no integrity. It was bad enough the way you left, but now you drag my good name through the mud? I will never understand why you did this to me. Never."

Whereas leaving Trent felt like nothing, wounding Scruggs felt like she'd just pushed someone she loved in front of a bus. She was so full of regret she could barely breathe.

He stopped before he got to the door. "Where are the flowers? Did you throw them away?"

"I still have them. Do you want them back?" They were the first thing she'd packed.

In a year, his face had grown sharper and this new expression was one she didn't remember seeing before. It was like there was a war going on behind his eyes: resignation versus fight, or maybe hope versus pain. Whatever it was, she had brutally hurt him. He hesitated before swinging open the door. "No."

Chapter Seven

EMMA WOKE UP dizzy. She didn't know if she was shaking from the fact that the bedroom was freezing or because something really, really bad was coming. Maybe it was because Christmas was only a couple of weeks away and she was completely alone. She had no plans, no gifts purchased, and not one decoration put up. That would make anyone feel sad. But it wasn't the sadness or loneliness that had her off-kilter. It was an overwhelming restlessness and feeling of dread.

Nights and mornings were cold in the house, and there was only a small stack of firewood by a wood stove in the family room downstairs. With her lack of knowledge about building fires, she might very well smoke herself out or burn down the house if she tried to light it. But she had to do something to make herself more comfortable. Her fingertips were turning blue.

She'd seen a thick light blue robe in the closet and a pair of slippers, so she put those on and trudged downstairs to make a hot cup of coffee, stopping at the foot of the stairs to check the front porch for an apple. There it was, round and unblemished. And, to her left, Brownie was saluting the flag. She waited until he put his hand down before shouting her greeting. "Good morning, Mr. Howell!"

He waved and smiled at her.

"Thanks for the apple!"

He gave her a thumbs-up.

"You ever catch that shark?"

He chuckled and shouted back, "Tryin' again today."

"Good luck!" she said. Something soft whispered past her ankle, and she saw a flash of orange fur run into the house. She followed it, closing the door behind her.

"Hey, you little stinker!"

The cat had gone straight up the stairs and was sniffing at the mirror in the alcove. When she approached, the fur on the ridge of his back stood straight up.

"Oh, come on," she said, kneeling in front of him. She put out her hand for the cat to smell. Sometimes that worked with animals. "If you can be nice, I might let you stay. It's cold out there this morning."

The cat was on full alert and poised to attack.

"Alrighty then." She pulled her hand back. "How about this? I'll go get some coffee, and when you see fit to come back downstairs, I'll let you out. Just don't pee in here, okay?"

Clearly, the cat did not appreciate her condescending tone of voice. He swatted at her, missing by a foot.

"That is not how you make friends," she said as she left.

At the kitchen table with her coffee, she set about googling how to light a wood stove when a headline caught her attention: TRENT BROADWAY'S OTHER WOMAN.

A tremble ran from head to foot. There it was. The reason why she woke up anxious. She clicked on the link, but she already knew whose name she would see associated with Trent's. She'd been suspicious of the two of them for a long time. Since before the wedding, actually. She scanned the story until she saw it: Abby Wingate.

Emma actually liked Abby. They'd been friends since elementary school. When Abby was a freshman in high school, her parents had divorced and something happened to her after that. There were rumors about her mental health, that she had tried to hurt herself. She was sent away for the whole summer to some sort of wilderness place for depressed people.

If memory served, Abby had left just as she and Trent were beginning to date. Then when she came back, her mom moved from Beaufort to Hilton Head and enrolled her in a private school out there. Every now and then Abby would come back to visit, and each time, she'd always see Trent. It made no difference back then because Emma wasn't dating him. She didn't date him until after college when their parents literally planned an entire party around getting the two of them together. But she'd always had a feeling Abby was still in his heart somewhere.

Now, according to the story, she'd been in more than

just his heart. She'd been in his car, in his office, and most recently, in the red-light decorated home Emma had just left. Despite the fact that Emma didn't want Trent at the moment, the photos felt like she'd been whacked in the face with a middle school yearbook—the one where Abby looked cute and Emma sported braces and a bad haircut.

The cat slinked past Emma to the back door and meowed with gusto.

"Fine, you little twerp," she said as she opened the back door for him. What a day. If it weren't so ridiculously cold, she would go back to bed. Her phone buzzed. It was Trent, of course. He'd probably just seen the headline.

"Hey," she answered.

"It's not true," he said.

"Don't even bother lying, Trent. I've pretty much known all along."

"I never did anything with her."

"Oh. So there's a picture of her from yesterday, leaving our house, but you didn't do anything with her."

"You know what I mean. We were just talking. This hasn't been easy on me. I needed someone to talk to."

"Easy on you? Give me a break. I am alone in a green igloo getting shunned by my parents."

He sighed loudly. "Can you focus on me for a second? I'm the one running for governor. This affects me more."

She laughed at his gall and sheer lack of awareness. "No. No, Trent, I can't. I am tired of focusing on you. Everything is always about you." Her voice grew progressively louder. "You acted all high and mighty about me and Scruggs, whom I *left* before we were married and *didn't speak to* again, when all along you've been talking to Abby."

"Talking!" he said. "That's all."

"Let's say for a second that you didn't do anything with her, okay? Let's pretend like I believe you. You may not have been having a physical affair, but you are having an emotional one."

"Those are just words, Emma Shea. I didn't cross a line."

"You crossed my line," she said.

"You are not going to turn this around on me. You understand? Now, I need you to meet with my team so we can manage this."

"Thank you for the kind invitation, but I will not be meeting with your team."

"Well, then meet with me, so we can figure out how to spin this. You have to cooperate. I mean it."

"What? You're my dad now? Like, I have to do what you say or you're going to ground me? You stole my money from our bank account. You accused me of something you yourself were doing. You kicked me out of our home."

"Technically, you left," he interjected.

"Screw you." She hung up on him for the second time. What a self-centered, entitled jerk. She sat in her frustration, staring blindly out the window at the back porch. The orange cat walked into view, flipped up his tail, squished his hindquarters downward, and left a steaming pile of excrement near her back stairs. He stared directly at her the entire time.

"You little—" she said, omitting the s-word, as she'd been taught that cussing was low class. Never mind lighting the wood stove. She had to get out of here. She would take a hot shower and head over to Tea and Tennyson where it was warm and the coffee tasted better.

EMMA MANAGED TO buy a coffee and a hot ham bun before Birdie made her usual dramatic entrance. "Y'all are probably wondering why I'm late," she said before the door even closed behind her. "I have been working all morning on my new video." She made it to the counter and waited for someone to respond.

One "Hi, Birdie" was all she got.

"Y'all not even gonna ask me what the video is about? Come on! At least pretend like you've got manners." She forcibly made eye contact with Charlotte, who was putting a plate of Christmas shortbread cookies in the case.

"What is the video about?" Charlotte asked sweetly.

Birdie laughed loudly. "I had Ashby acting like he was somebody's paw-paw all morning. Lordy! This is gonna be one of my best videos yet. I'm calling it *How to Keep Yourself in Granddaddy's Will—Christmas Edition*." She looked around the store, smiling at every head that turned to listen. "Everybody knows rule number one: Always act like it's the first time you've heard the story. Nod and laugh, that's all you've got to do. Nod and laugh. And feel free to add in an *Oh, Paw-Paw, you're so funny* for extra credit."

"Sounds like a good one," Charlotte said.

"Mrs. Broadway, or whatever the hell your name is now," Birdie called out. "Do you know rule number two?"

A gentleman holding a book looked up. Emma shook her head at Birdie.

"If Grandpa is losing his mind, treat him just like you would someone who says a curse word—ignore the offense and react only to what you are willing to hear."

As Birdie was talking, the man made his way to Emma's table.

"Excuse me, ma'am. May I speak with you?"

Emma didn't answer. Who was he?

"I work for an online publication, and I would like to ask you some questions about Trent Broadway."

"No thank you," Emma said, shaking her head.

The man didn't leave. "I don't mean to be rude, but this is a public place and I am within my rights to snap some photos of you."

"What?" Was he serious? Could that be true?

As if demonstrating the truth of his proclamation, he lifted his phone and took a photo right there and then. "Did you know your husband was cheating on you with Abby

Wingate?"

By the time Emma said "Please leave me alone," Birdie had already swooped in.

"Get your ass out of here, you nasty piece of trash. Who do you think you are coming in here and harassing a guest?" She positioned her body between him and Emma.

"I am a paying customer."

"And I am a pissed-off old lady. You don't want to mess with me."

He stepped to the side, as if he was going to leave. Then turned back around and snapped another photo of Emma. "Are you gonna get back with him?" he asked. "Do you even care that he's cheating? Or are you just dead set on being this state's first lady? You wanna live in that big historic house in Beaufort and be the belle of the ball, don't you?"

Emma's mouth dropped. How could he say such things?

"Stop taunting her! If she wanted to be the frickin' first lady, she wouldn't have left the douchebag." Birdie put her hands on his chest and attempted to physically push him toward the front. Thankfully, the man moved. Charlotte held the door open for him, but before he stepped outside, he spun out of Birdie's grasp and ran back to Emma, snapping photos along the way.

"Ow!" Birdie screamed, holding her left wrist. "You stupid man! I am going to skin your hide!"

Footsteps came hurriedly down the back stairs, and Scruggs appeared, running toward Birdie. "Birdie! Are you okay?"

"That man"—she used her good hand to point—"has injured me and is harassing our Emma."

Scruggs held a hammer in his hand as he stomped toward the man, who was taking pictures as quickly as he could.

"Are you Scruggs Willingham?" The man was gleeful. He didn't care a lick that he was the most hated man in the room at the moment. "When was the last time you slept with Emma Shea Broadway?"

They'd never slept together. They'd only fallen in love. Scruggs raised the hammer over his head and raced toward the man, who finally found his sense and ran out the still-open front door. Scruggs stood with the hammer at the ready as they all watched the man sprint down the street like a sleazy, greedy criminal.

Emma ran to Birdie. "Are you okay?" she asked. "I'm so sorry!"

"It's not your fault there are assholes in the world," she said.

Scruggs put down the hammer and gently examined Birdie's wrist. "Looks like a sprain," he said, before turning his attention to Emma. "You okay?"

She nodded. "I just feel horrible." She had no control over the shaking. She should have known better than to go out in public. Scruggs gently placed Birdie's wrist onto the ice pack in Charlotte's hands, then, surprisingly, pulled

Emma in for a quick hug. She was so caught off guard that she was stiff and forgot to hug him back.

"This will pass," he said. "You're gonna be okay."

His kindness, his utter selflessness was such a departure from anyone else in her life. The smell of him, the familiarity, the nearness, brought all of the old feelings flooding back.

The reporter was right. Her desire to be the belle of the ball had ruined the best thing she'd ever had.

Chapter Eight

B Y THE NEXT morning, the balmy winter weather was back. Emma was relieved the orange cat would be warm, although she didn't know why. He was nothing but ornery and rude to her. She'd slept in later than usual and was disappointed that she missed Brownie flying the colors. When she saw the flag up and waving in the breeze, she did a little salute before picking up her apple.

The kitchen was beginning to smell like coffee as it percolated into the pot. She propped open the porch door, sat on a rocking chair, and texted her mother.

"Hey, Mama. You okay?" She wanted to say, *Christmas is coming up and if you had any spine at all, you would show some love and support to your one-and-only daughter.* But regardless of Emma's good manners and sweetness, the three little dots of reply never appeared. The message, like most of the others, went into the abyss.

"Fine," she said out loud. "Fine. Fine. Fine."

A little orange face looked down at her from the roof.

"There you are, ya surly little grouch. You want to hiss at me? Fine. You want to poop on my porch? Fine. I don't care about you or Mama or the stupid media or Trent or anybody anymore. I am fine by myself." She pulled up the Louis Vuitton website, scrolled through some three-thousand-dollar bags, then immediately X'd out of it. She didn't even want another stupid purse. She looked down at her borrowed blue bathrobe and slippers. They belonged to one of her grandmothers, they kept her warm, and they were more valuable at that moment than any designer bag.

The coffee was ready, so she poured a cup and sipped as she diced her apple and fried it up with a little butter, sugar, and cinnamon. It smelled like the holidays, which for a moment felt nostalgic, until she quickly remembered that Christmas this year was going to be lonely, tradition-free, and present-free. She cinched her bathrobe tightly and put her breakfast on the tray. When she opened the door to the porch, she nearly dropped it all when the cat suddenly appeared at her feet and ran inside like something was chasing him.

"Again?!" She put down the tray and turned around to follow him. He went straight up the stairs and sat by the mirror in the alcove. Having learned her lesson, she closed the door to the bedroom so he couldn't get in and pee in her bed or poop on the carpet. Then she left him alone and went back downstairs to finish her breakfast, leaving the back door open so he could escape when he was ready. "Danged cat." She shook her head.

She was three bites in when the doorbell rang. Rather

than a peephole, there was a little square door built into the thick front door. She unlatched it and looked through, coming face-to-face with Trent. Of course he would catch her on a day when she'd slept in and was still in her pajamas. She shouldn't have opened the tiny door.

"We need to talk," he said.

She couldn't avoid him forever. And the truth was, she didn't hate him. She didn't want to ruin his career. She just didn't want to be married to him. She unlocked the big door and let him in.

He followed her to the kitchen table. "Weird that your mama has this place and never told you."

"I know," she said, shrugging. "That's my family for you; we're all about secrets and suspicion."

He looked at her strangely, and Emma realized that she had never said anything derogatory to him about her family before. She'd spent her whole life playing a role and doing her part to create a facade of perfection.

"Have you seen the news?" he asked.

She sat at the kitchen table, but he was clearly too wound up to relax. "No. But after what happened yesterday, I have a pretty good idea of what pictures they're posting."

"Your dude had a hammer." His eyes stopped on the vase of flowers made from brightly colored Legos adorning the center of the table. She'd unpacked and set them up last night.

Emma sucked in her breath. "Oh no. They posted that

one? I thought it would be of me." Her heart sank. Scruggs didn't deserve to have his reputation tarnished again, especially when he'd been standing up for her—or for Birdie, really.

"What in the hell were you thinking?" His nostrils flared, and Emma knew where the conversation was headed. "Are you trying to keep this crap going? Because every time they find something to talk about, it always comes back to me." He was still escalating, and he'd probably been stewing on the hour-long drive to find her. He wouldn't stop until he blew. "People are gonna start thinking that I can't run a state if I can't control my own fucking wife."

A loud, angry meow came from upstairs. Trent looked toward the stairs.

"Don't mind him," she said.

"Is someone here?" He growled the question like he suspected her of planting a reporter in the upstairs bedroom.

"It's only a cat."

He appeared confused. Emma's family weren't exactly animal lovers. As a matter of fact, their two-story den had mounted heads of animals ranging from a moose to three different kinds of bears. She couldn't help but smile at the fact that her old blue robe and tiny green house complete with boisterous cat had shocked him.

"Wipe that smile off your face," he said. "This is my life we are talking about."

"It's my life, too, Trent. And we made a mistake. Now,

let's sit together like two adults and talk about it."

He paced the room, his long body and dark oiled hair making him look like a pent-up jaguar. Before she could react, he grabbed the Lego flowers from the table and threw them out the back door. They exploded into pieces all over the porch. "Shit!" he screamed. "Do you know how they're spinning this? Like he is some superhero protecting you from me!" He slammed his hands onto the table. "And some bird lady is all over the place talking about how great he is. And you know what? She says she's a close friend of yours."

He leaned in, his face far too close to hers, his breathing erratic, his lips white. "Did you do this, Emma Shea? Did you send in your loudmouth friend to make me look bad?"

A figure darkened the open porch doorway. "What's going on in here?" It was Brownie, his shoulders back as far as they would go, his stance wide and firm. She could see how he once would have been intimidating.

"Nothing's going on in here, old man," Trent said.

Brownie stepped inside. He wore khaki pants pulled up too high and a Wallace plaid flannel tucked in all the way up to the pockets. He was a full two feet shorter than Trent and a hundred times wrinklier. "I'll have you know," he said. "I am a veteran of two wars. I may not look like much, but I know how to fight."

Trent laughed. "I am not going to fight an old man."

"You mess with Miss Emma and you're not gonna have a choice." He held up his fists near his nose like a boxer.

"I am talking to my wife," Trent said. "This is none of your business."

"Do you want to talk to him?" Brownie asked her.

She didn't want to talk to him, but she also didn't want Brownie to get hurt. "It's okay," she said, moving her way between the two men. If Trent so much as pushed Brownie, he might break the man's hip. "Trent. I will handle Birdie, and I will fix this."

He looked over her head at Brownie, then back at her. "I'll call you this afternoon, and I expect things to have changed."

"Trust me," she said.

Trent grabbed his keys from the table and walked toward the front door.

"And don't come back!" Brownie yelled.

Trent flipped him off and slammed the door behind him.

Emma turned to Brownie. "Thank you," she said.

His saggy face broke into the largest, most endearing crooked-toothed grin she'd ever seen. "That felt real good," he said. "I sure showed him."

She hugged him tight, his body warm and squishy soft. "You sure did."

"I don't like you being out here by yourself," he said. "You can always call on me, you know. Neighbors have to look out for each other."

"Thank you," she repeated. "And if you ever need anything, I'm here for you, too."

"I know you are, doll." He winked at her. The orange cat chose that moment to saunter downstairs. "Ah, Louie. I see you've met Emma."

The cat ignored him and walked, tail up and full of sass, out the door.

"Is he yours?" she asked.

"Louie belongs to no man. Keeps himself fed and entertained by terrorizing the neighborhood. He's got to be older than Methuselah by now."

So, Louie was the cat's name. Emma had to laugh. Instead of a new Louis bag, she got a ratty old Louie cat.

"Listen," he said, following the cat out the door, "if you want more apples, you help yourself to my tree anytime."

"You are the best, Mr. Howell."

He grinned again, and her heart swelled to see him happy.

"If you're not doing anything for Christmas Eve," she said, "would you like to come here for dinner?" She hadn't really thought ahead about it, but he always seemed to be alone, and extending the invitation felt right.

"Well, now, my family is coming to me like they always do, but we would love for you to join us instead."

So, he had family. "Oh no. I don't want to interfere. I just thought that if you were going to be alone, then—"

"Then we could be lonely together?" he said. "You are joining us, and I won't take no for an answer. Walk on over around noon and bring your appetite."

It was clearly an order.

"There's only one rule," he said. "Every year my daughter brings that awful ambrosia salad. She does it for me—thinks I still like wartime food after all these years. If you are going to be a part of this family, you have got to eat the ambrosia and pretend like you like it."

A part of Brownie's family. She would happily eat ambrosia salad every day for the rest of her life if it meant being a part of anything associated with Brown Odgers Howell. "Yes, sir. I will eat it, and I will love it."

"Yes, you will," he said, gripping the handrail as he slowly took the back stairs. When he reached the bottom he turned around and waved.

"Thank you again!" she said, suddenly feeling inspired to set out some Christmas decorations. Maybe there was an attic in the old house that held something festive. Walking upstairs, she checked all of the ceilings for a crawl space but found nothing. She stood in the alcove, deciding where to look next, when she noticed that the full-length mirror the cat always ran straight to didn't actually touch the wood floor beneath it. There was a dark space.

She pulled up the flashlight app on her phone and did her best to look underneath. All she could see was more empty space. Strange. She put her fingers on the edge of the frame and pulled, but it didn't budge. She checked all around for a latch. Still nothing.

Looking closer at the frame, she noticed nails covered with a slightly mismatched white paint. They were only on the right side. She wished there was someone in the house she could yell to, someone to be with her. The feeling that she was on the verge of discovering something big was strong. She ran into the carport and rifled around until she found an old rusty tool chest that held a hammer. Then she ran back upstairs, taking care not to trip on the edge of her robe, and used the claw end of the hammer to pull out the nails.

She took a quick break to set up her phone to record whatever was about to happen. If she discovered a nest of giant spiders or a torture chamber or a portal to another dimension, someone might want to know how she died.

Then she pried loose the last nail.

Chapter Nine

TWO STEPS LED down into whatever the space was behind the mirror. It was as black and deep as a cave in there, and it smelled like one, too—cold and untouched. Emma felt around for a light switch, and when her fingers touched the familiar shape, she flipped it up and down several times before the lights flickered on. She sucked in her breath so hard that she nearly fell backward. It was like discovering the Cave of Wonders.

She'd found a secret room, and it was filled with treasures.

Emma walked into the space like she'd fallen into a trance, nearly tripping down the two wide stairs. There was so much to take in. Four crystal chandeliers hung in a row from the coffered ceiling with the inset lined in stamped bronze metal. A long bar lined the wall to the left, with a black stone top and wooden cabinetry painted a blue that matched the leather tufted-back barstools. It was the strangest, most beautiful blue—not light, not navy, not greenish or little boy-ish, but a cerulean sort of cobalt blue. Seating areas dotted the room with high tops in the center and lounge spaces in the corners.

There was no alcohol left on the shelves behind the bar, but it was clear that the space had once held plenty. A large gold sign read THE FIREFLY CLUB. It looked like one of the trendy speakeasies she'd seen popping up in every big city—retro yet modern. Only what she'd found was dusty, cracking in some places, and one hundred percent authentic.

Not only had Crazy Frannie been a bootlegger, she'd held illegal parties in this very room.

Emma walked through the space, touching every surface and leaving fingerprints in the dust, until she got to a white Christmas tree made from sun-bleached oyster shells. It was as tall as she was, with a gold star on top. A sign next to it read MERRY CHRISTMAS 1933. Was the loopy cursive her great-great-grandmother's handwriting? Emma's hands shook as she googled Christmas 1933. The first thing that popped up was "December 5, 1933 21st Amendment is Ratified; Prohibition Ends." Her heart pounded.

Did her mother know about it? Emma misspelled words as her head spun with excitement.

"Mama, dd you konw about the secret roomm? The one behnd the mirror?"

Her mother responded immediately. *"Don't mess with me."*

Emma took several pictures and sent them.

"OH MY WORD," her mother wrote.

"It's The Firefly Club," Emma replied. She sat on one of

the corner couches and took it all in. The crepe myrtle out front, the one that used to have twinkle lights, had beckoned people to the house at 19 Blue Ghost Lane. Blue ghost was a nickname for fireflies.

She imagined her great-great-grandmother managing it all in its heyday. She didn't know much about the era, but she did know it was during the Great Depression, and that Frannie's husband had died. Is this how she made her money, how she kept herself afloat? Emma had so many questions.

She wandered around the room for three full hours, and with each passing minute she felt stronger, more renewed. The blood of Frances Mackey ran through her veins—she shared DNA with a woman who wasn't held down by convention and societal rules about what women were and were not allowed to do. A woman who didn't need a big fancy house in order to feel valuable, who didn't need a man to take care of her. It was time for Emma to create a new beginning, to be her own light, and to find her own way.

After a hot shower and a quick sandwich, Emma was going to drive to Beaufort. She envisioned herself marching up the cracked marble stairs and knocking on the door of the home she'd lived in for the past year. She was going to tell Trent exactly how things were going to go. She was going to be the boss.

She'd stepped into the secret room for one more look before leaving when her phone dinged with a text message from Charlotte.

"I'm adding you to a group text. Sorry for the late notice, but I know Krista would want you to be there."

The group message included Scruggs, Birdie, and several other numbers without names attached.

It said: *"It's almost time for Krista's big surprise! Do your best to make it. No need to dress up. Tea and Tennyson, 3 p.m."*

Well, that changed things. She felt honored that they'd thought to include her. She was about to ask if she needed to bring a gift when another text came through.

"No gifts."

Although just a moment before she was filled with confidence and momentum, she was suddenly tired and overwhelmingly anxious about going to Krista's surprise party alone, especially if Scruggs was going to be there. Immediately, she began making up excuses. It was supposed to rain that afternoon. She had nothing to wear. If it was a birthday surprise, she was probably supposed to bring a gift even though she was told not to, and there was no time to shop.

The Moroccan-shaped champagne-colored tile back-splash at the bar reflected the light from the chandeliers, and her attention was pulled back to the room. If Crazy Frannie had done the decorating herself, she'd been a woman of talent and vision. The space was too beautiful to be kept hidden away for all of those years. Emma should be the one having a party. The room demanded it. It had been a place for people to gather during a very difficult time in the history of the country. And it wasn't done yet.

"Oh," Emma said to the room. "I see. People need to get together. It doesn't matter what we wear or what we bring, we just need to be together."

CHARLOTTE MET EVERYONE at the door, handed them a rose, and scuttled them to the back of the store. "Try to blend in so she doesn't notice you," she said.

It was great to have a job to do. Emma took a table for two by the nonfiction section and grabbed a book, pretending to read. She hid the rose next to her thigh on the chair.

Scruggs walked in and looked around. There was only one empty seat in the entire store, and it happened to be directly across from Emma. He looked stiff and awkward as he appraised his options before sucking it up and walking over to her table.

"Hey," he said. "You mind?"

She shook her head, hyper-aware of his nearness as he sat. Immediately, she had butterflies. It was just like when she was working at Tea and Tennyson and dating him.

"How ya doin?" he asked.

"Fine." She smiled briefly, her nose in the book. It was still hard for her to understand, but during the time she dated Scruggs, her two lives felt completely separate. She had a life in Crickley Creek and a life in Beaufort, and if she didn't think about it too much, she could keep them separate and therefore keep doing it. Keep cheating, keep lying—none of which she'd admitted to herself she was doing at the time.

"How are you?" she asked him.

He shrugged, and she remembered too clearly the messages he'd left on her phone after she left. His voice growing increasingly worried, then angry, and then simply filled with pain and sadness as he asked where she was, then whether she was coming back, and why she wasn't returning his calls. And then the final question—*who even are you?*

"I've been meaning to say thanks for helping me out the other day," she said. "I just didn't want to call or text you in case your girlfriend would get mad."

"Yeah," he said, flipping his bangs to the right. "Well, I guess my hammer made the news." He laughed, and she was relieved.

"Hey, Scruggs?" she began. She'd rehearsed a heartfelt apology a million times since the day she left. But what began as a list of excuses had recently morphed into things she was grateful for. Like, the fact that he'd shown her there was another kind of a man in the world—the kind who wasn't concerned with appearances, the kind who did things out of genuine concern rather than for the accolades. As Scruggs sat in front of her in his wrinkly button-down, she felt a deep wave of admiration. It was a small miracle that he was even talking to her. She didn't deserve for him to be so kind. "I've been wanting to tell you—" she began.

Charlotte whistled, getting everyone's attention. Birdie ran for the chair she'd saved with her oversized purse like the music had just stopped and she needed to win the prize. Emma still had Scruggs's full attention, but her eyes were drawn to the front door where Krista was entering, followed by her tall, athletic boyfriend, Johnny.

A little girl ran up to Krista and hugged her legs. "Andy Sue!" Krista exclaimed. "What are you doing here?"

Andy Sue handed her big sister a pink rose.

"What's this for?" She raised her eyes to the rest of the room in time for each person she knew to stand one at a time, make their way to her, and present her with a rose.

The look of astonishment on her face was extremely gratifying.

"What on earth?" Krista laughed. "It is not my birthday, y'all."

While she was facing the crowd in the bookstore, Johnny, who was behind her, got down on one knee. When the last rose was delivered, Krista turned around to look for him. She gasped when she saw him and immediately joined him on the ground. Johnny hadn't even gotten to the question before she leaned into him.

"Yes!"

He asked the question anyway, and after she'd sung a chorus of yeses, he put a sparkling ring on her finger, lifted her off the ground, and kissed her.

Every face in the room was smiling. Emma stole a look at Scruggs, and his eyes were bright and moist. She immediately turned her head when he caught her looking, but from the corner of her eye, she could tell he was punching something into his phone. A second later, Bruno Mars sang "Marry You" from every speaker in the place.

"Perfect!" Krista said, waving to Scruggs through her tears. She and Johnny were surrounded by all of the people they loved the most, and the hugs seemed like they would never end.

It was pretty much the opposite of when Emma had gotten engaged. She'd known it was coming and had bought a dress especially for the occasion. A professional photographer was hired and every moment had been posed. What looked like a dream come true had actually been nothing more than an emotionless, stressful photo shoot. They even sat and waited, sweating in the heat of summer, until the golden hour was just right. Then her makeup was professionally touched up, she turned on a smile, and they both did their best to pretend like they had what everyone wanted: true love.

Krista and Johnny were what true love looked like. Charlotte and Will, too. What Emma had was a farce.

And she had no one to blame but herself.

Every Southern girl has a convincing fake smile and Emma used hers generously as she clapped for Krista and

Johnny. It wasn't that she wasn't happy for them. She was. But she was beginning to understand that driving her car to Beaufort and picking a fight with Trent over money and reputation and who-did-what, plus a thousand piddly things she so desperately wanted to blame him for probably wasn't the right thing to do either. The impromptu engagement party had saved her from yet another mistake. She needed to get her life back on track by being thoughtful and reasonable. She needed to take a step back and assess the situation with a clear mind. After all, she hadn't been the only miserable person in her marriage.

That gave her an idea.

Chapter Ten

A TRIP TO Beaufort was back in order, only this time the purpose was to speak with Trent about her idea, and to pick up some casual clothes that she desperately needed. She'd been surviving on designer dresses and borrowed outdated ensembles from various bygone eras. She sipped her coffee on the back porch and kept an eye out for Louie as she mentally prepared herself for whatever might happen. Friends, neighbors, the press—if she ran into any of them, she would paste a smile on her face and go on about her business. She was only going to her own home, anyway. She wasn't breaking any rules. Plus, how many people would she realistically see?

When she pulled up to the historic Classic Revival home, the first thing she noticed was that the Christmas lights were on in the middle of the day. That was a waste of electricity and would be frowned upon by the neighborhood committee. The next thing she noticed was that the lights were not the red ones she'd chosen but had been replaced with the white icicle kind. The kind Trent preferred. She'd been gone one week and he'd already changed out the lights? Had he paid another five hundred dollars? And which bank account did he take it from? Her resolve to be peaceful was quickly disintegrating.

She carefully stepped around the dented marble in the center of the front steps and looked ahead at the tall front windows symmetrically placed on either side of the front door. In the parlor to the left, seated on her newly reupholstered wing chair, was her father. He was supposed to be in Florida with her mother. This was one scenario she was absolutely not prepared for. Her daddy was visiting Trent behind her back?

She knew immediately what he was doing: choosing sides against his daughter.

Her knees nearly buckled. She wanted to turn tail and run back to safety, back to the little green house on the beach. She had never stood up to her father, and never would. She jumped across the cracked portion of the steps to the other side, where they couldn't see her, and watched as her mother walked into the room. She held a glass of brown liquid, most likely the six-hundred-dollar bourbon that Trent saved to impress people, and handed it to her husband. So, on top of his presence in her home, her father would soon be drunk, too. It was no longer safe for her to be here, especially hunched like a frightened mouse on the front steps.

"Hey," came a voice from the sidewalk.

She was practically deaf with fear, so the sound only registered once she stood on the sidewalk directly in front of Abby Wingate.

"Hey," Emma said, out of breath. "Thanks for coming."

"You okay?" she asked, pulling her shoulders back, which made her several inches taller than Emma.

"Guess I've got to make an appointment to go to my own home these days."

"These are strange times for sure," Abby agreed.

The two women stood in silence, neither of them moving until Emma remembered that she couldn't have her father see her. She wasn't ready for that confrontation yet, or ever. "How about we meet without Trent first? I can't go inside right now."

Abby looked as unbothered and sanguine as ever. "Sure. What'd you have in mind?"

"Coffee?" Emma asked. "Or is Trent expecting you?"

"He won't miss me," she said. "Let's go get that coffee."

"Hop in." Emma already had the passenger door open. There was no time to overthink, so she just had to follow her heart.

The two women sped off down the road.

WHEN EMMA FINALLY returned to the beach from her crazy unexpected day in Beaufort, a middle-aged woman with dyed blonde hair, layers of makeup, and a perfectly tailored suit jacket was sitting at the kitchen table next to the clear vase filled with Lego bricks that used to be in the shape of flowers. "Mama? What are you doing here?"

"I saw you in Beaufort today," she said, barely making eye contact with her daughter.

"You're supposed to be in Florida." Emma used her sassiest voice to show her mother how incensed she was. They'd lied to her!

"Your father says the bugs are as big as the alligators in Florida. You know that."

So, I'm the stupid one for believing your lie? Emma bit her tongue. Her whole life she'd been made to feel like everything she said or did was wrong. "How did you get away from him?" she asked.

Clarissa Abernathy gazed past her daughter like she wasn't there. "I handed him his bourbon, and I told him that was the last one he'd ever have served by me." With a *thunk*, she placed her elbows on the table and held her head in her hands for several seconds before raising her head again, still dry-eyed. "Some nice person on the street called me a driver. I believe his name was Uber."

Emma was already making sure the front door was locked. Then she locked the door to the porch. "Daddy is not going to be happy. Does he know where this place is?"

Clarissa nodded.

"There's a neighbor named Brownie next door. Maybe we should call him."

"Old Mr. Howell? Oh yes. Let's call him." The way she drew out the words made it clear that she had no faith in that plan.

"Daddy won't let you leave him."

"Well, he doesn't have a choice now, does he?" The words were strong, but her hunched shoulders told a different story. She stood and opened a cupboard, pulled out a glass, and filled it with water from the pitcher in the refrigerator. It was strange the way she knew her way around the kitchen. She was comfortable, like the home really did belong to her.

"How long have you been coming here, Mama?"

Clarissa took a sip. "Oh, too many years to count. Shared it with my mother for a long time before she passed. Every woman needs a safe place to hide out. It will be yours one of these days."

Every woman needs a safe place to hide out? That was so messed up. It didn't need to be that way. "Mama—"

"Emma Shea. If you're thinking about lecturing me—don't." She sighed loudly and slumped back into the same chair, holding on to her water glass like it was filled with her tears. "I don't know if I have it in me to spend Christmas without him."

"Come here, Mama. Let me show you something." Emma tried to coax her mother up by pulling gently on her arm.

Her mother wriggled away. "If you're going to show me that secret room you're so excited about, I do not want to see it."

"It's decorated for Christmas. And it's beautiful. I think you'll feel better when you see it."

"Do you know what it's like to think you know something, to believe that you have an understanding of a place where you have spent many difficult times, to trust that there is one place in your life that holds no surprises?" The righteous indignation in her voice was at least a little bit forceful. "It is quite disconcerting to be wrong."

Emma sat down at the table with her. "I understand what you're saying, but I think you'll really like it."

"I will be sleeping downstairs," her mother said. "I refuse to be anywhere near that room."

There was a loud knock at the door, and both women jumped. "Mama, hide!" she said quietly but with force. "I'll tell him you're not here."

Clarissa didn't move.

"Mama!" Emma did her best to pull her mother up by the arm. "Go out the back. Run over to Brownie's house. Get out of here!"

The knock came again, louder. This time, Clarissa stood. "Umm," she whispered. Then she tiptoed to the front stairs and dashed up. When she reached the alcove, Emma watched her hesitate before entering the hidden room and closing the mirrored door behind her.

Emma opened the small door-within-a-front-door and peered out, trying to keep her face passive despite her heart drumming up into her throat. The person standing there was not who she expected.

"Has she come to her senses yet?" Brownie asked.

"Not yet," Emma said, her shoulders dropping with relief. "But I'm working on it." She opened the door for him to enter. "Mama!" she yelled up the stairs. "It's Mr. Howell!"

It took a few seconds before a sticky sweet voice yelled back, "Oh, lovely. Please join me up here, Mr. Howell!"

Emma led the way, but climbing the stairs was not an easy task for Brownie. It took time and rest breaks, but he managed it without complaint. The look on his face when he reached the room was worth every step. "I have…I have never…this is…" He put a hand to his heart as he stepped inside. "Frances Mackey. This room is her." His watery eyes nearly overflowed. "That woman," he said with love and respect as he placed his thick, wrinkly hands on the cold stone of the bar. "She never told me this was here. Never said one word."

He shuffled around the room with a wistful smile. "She was a friend to my wife, you know. Taught her how to love me is what she did. Convinced her not to cut the line on this big old shark but to fight it out instead." He wiped his eyes with his flannel sleeve. "There are times for both, you know."

He focused on Clarissa, sitting in the far corner. "Hello, doll. You're back."

She nodded. "I hope you have some apples on your tree

for me."

"You bet I do." He smiled, taking in the room again. "Not many things surprise me anymore, but this surely does."

"Isn't it perfect?" When Clarissa spoke the words, she sounded like a little girl.

Emma experienced the warmest, most welcome relief. It was hard not to say *I told you so*. The room was a gift. An unexpected, much-needed gift.

"And it's already decorated for Christmas," Emma pointed out.

"Perfect timing," Brownie said, inspecting every shelf, every chair, every oyster shell glued onto the large round triangular frame with the glittery gold star on top. "Frannie did all this. She planned this surprise for you from the great beyond. That broad is still powerful." He laughed as he spoke to the room at large. "I'm on to you, Frannie. I know what you're doing."

Chapter Eleven

E MMA AWOKE WITH the sun the next morning. It was going to be a warm day, and she planned to spend it outside. She would put twinkle lights on the old cinnamon crepe myrtle out front, just like Frannie had done. Then she'd rifle through an old tin recipe box she'd found in the kitchen and see if she could bake up a family dish or two. Aside from oyster stew on Christmas Eve, there hadn't been much in the way of family traditions growing up, and she suddenly felt highly motivated to start some.

She practically skipped down the steps, excited to start the coffee brewing and greet her mother with breakfast in bed. She'd had an epiphany as she was falling asleep, happily secure with her mother in the house downstairs. If the speakeasy was The Firefly Club, then they were the Firefly Girls. She absolutely adored the name.

Certainly, with the overgrown plants out front, fireflies were abundant in the warm months, blinking out from the dark spaces behind the big, green elephant ears and all around the airy ferns. So in the winter months she would replicate them with lights. And, like those little lightning bugs, she and her mother would bring themselves out of darkness with lights of their own. Little yellow lights of hope. Emma poured two mugs full of coffee and felt weightless enough to fly.

Grabbing the black tray with the painted-on Gullah words, she placed a plate, a fork, and a napkin. Maybe her mother knew what the saying meant. *Hunnuh mus tek cyear a de root fah heal de tree.* Something about healing a tree. When the frozen biscuits were fluffy and golden brown, she split them apart and covered both sides with butter and honey.

Things were definitely looking up. She might get to spend Christmas with her mother, she'd almost gotten to apologize to Scruggs, and she'd had a great talk with Abby— a talk that played into her plan perfectly. Even grumpy orange Louie sat calmly on the back porch stairs staring out at the sea as if all was well in his world, too.

The only thing she needed to complete the breakfast were some slices of fresh apple. Opening the front door, she fully expected to see two of them waiting for her. One for her and one for her mother. But the little table was empty. Brownie must have forgotten. She balanced the tray as she knocked on her mother's door. "Mama? I brought you breakfast."

There was no answer.

She knocked again. "Mama? You awake?"

Still no answer, so she opened the door. The iron bed

was perfectly made, a patchwork quilt folded neatly at the bottom. Not a soul was in the room. Emma put down the tray and checked the bathroom. She yelled, "Mama?" And when there was still no answer, she ran out front to see if her mother's car was there before remembering that she'd taken an Uber.

She pulled her phone from the pocket of the blue robe. There wasn't even a message. Her mother had left without a word. Why was she even surprised? Her mother choosing her father over her was the story of her life. She suddenly felt as empty as the little table by the front door. Which reminded her. Had Brownie flown the flag that morning? She ran back to the front to check.

The flagpole was empty.

Panic engulfed her. Forgetting to shut her own door, she ran across the driveway to his house and rang his doorbell insistently. She waited a few seconds, then knocked. When there was no answer, she knocked again so hard that her knuckles hurt, then rang the doorbell over and over and over again. "Brownie!" she yelled. "Mr. Howell!" She jiggled the door handle, but it was locked. Cupping her hands against the glass, she peered into the front window, but the living room was empty. She ran around to the back of the house and tried the back door. It swung open on the first try. "Mr. Howell?" she yelled into the house. "Brownie? Are you okay?" His home was much bigger than hers, and she didn't know which way to go.

"In here," came a deep, groggy voice.

She followed the sound around to the right and found Brownie sitting in a dark-brown recliner looking stunned, different. His face sagged more than normal. "I can't get up," he said, each word slurred, slow and drawn out.

She ran to him. "Oh, Brownie." His hand was freezing as she took it in hers. "I'm calling 911." She dialed the numbers and explained what she knew, wondering if it was okay to say to the operator what she thought had happened. She didn't want to scare or misdiagnose him. But she needed to give all the information she could.

"I think he's had a stroke."

When she was assured that an ambulance was on its way, she turned her attention back to her beloved neighbor. "Are you in pain?" she asked, covering him with a nearby knit blanket.

With effort, he slurred, "You look good, Frannie."

"I'm Emma," she said.

"Did my wife tell you that she's pregnant?" he asked, managing to lift one hand and put a shaky finger to his lips. "Shhhh. It's still early." His eyes twinkled like his brain hadn't just been terribly damaged. "I'm gonna be a daddy."

"I'm so happy for you," Emma said, gently holding his hand. There was no use arguing. "You are going to be the best daddy."

"Family," he said. "That's all I want in this whole world." A stream of saliva escaped from the corner of his downturned lips.

"And you're going to have a great one," she said. "You will be so loved."

He nodded. "I am blessed." The *b* was difficult for him.

"You certainly are."

The first note of sirens could be heard in the distance. "Help is on the way," she said. "Is there anyone I should call?"

"Naw. Don't worry my wife. I'll be home soon, good as new."

Emma nodded. "Okay." She wasn't going to argue with him or remind him that his wife had been deceased for well over thirty years. When the sirens stopped in front of his house, she let the medical professionals in the front door and held tight to his hand after they strapped him onto the gurney, walking with him to the vehicle. She kissed his cheek before they rolled him into the open back doors. "I love you, Brownie," she said when she was forced to let go.

"You're a good person, Frannie."

Once the EMTs closed the doors and took off down the road, Emma ran inside her house. She had to shower, get dressed, and drive to the hospital. She would be there for him in the waiting room. Even if it turned out that he had a million nearby relatives who all wanted to see him, she would still be there—either as Frannie or as Emma. It didn't matter.

Something about the hot shower made her tears flow. By

the time she was clean and dry, she was all cried out. There was still the daily problem of having no casual clothes to wear, so she rummaged around many eras of old clothes until she found a pair of navy-blue pants, a white short-sleeved blouse, and tan sandals. It may be nearing the end of December, but it was going to be close to eighty degrees in Crickley Creek today.

She forced herself to take bites of a biscuit and drink some coffee, even though it didn't sound good at all. There was no telling how long she'd be in the waiting room and whether there would be food available.

Grabbing her designer bag from the counter, she dug for her keys and walked out the front door. What she saw in Brownie's front yard brought her to a halt, her jaw hanging open.

She would recognize the person she saw there anywhere. Even from behind. It was Scruggs. He was in Brownie's yard, saluting a half-mast flag.

"Scruggs!" she cried.

He turned around quickly. "Emma? What are you doing here?"

"I've been staying in this house." She swept her hand toward it. "Do you know Brownie?"

"Of course I do. He's my grandfather."

"What?" She was frozen until instantaneous hiccups, tears, and a full-on runny-nosed hysteria took her over right there in the front yard of number 19 Blue Ghost Lane.

"Hey," Scruggs said, running to her.

She bent over, hands on knees, hyperventilating.

He rubbed her back. "He's gonna be okay," he said. "Mama said he's already showing signs of recovery, and there are medications."

Emma's words came out in between breaths. "I. Can't. Believe. Brownie. Is. Your. Grandfather."

Scruggs chuckled. "In all his glory. The first demand he made at the hospital was that someone come here and fly his flag. He been leaving you apples?"

She nodded.

"Yeah," Scruggs said, "he has way more than he can eat, and he likes to be generous without people knowing. It'd blow his grumpy old man cover."

"I need to wipe my face," she squeaked, hoping her mascara wasn't running in streaks to her chin. He followed her inside her little house as she grabbed a handful of tissues from the downstairs bathroom.

"Are you the one who called the ambulance?" he asked.

She nodded, blowing her nose.

"Thanks for that," he said. "I don't like thinking about what might've happened if you didn't figure it out."

"I would've called you, too, if I'd known."

They stood outside the bathroom door in the hallway, their proximity to each other still hotly palpable despite the circumstances. "So that must have been kinda scary. You know, finding him like that. You okay?"

She nodded. "I thought he was dead," she said, wiping at fresh tears. "I wasn't ready. I won't ever be ready for that. I really care about him."

"Come here." He stepped forward and hugged her to his chest. They stood that way until her erratic pulse calmed to match the steady rhythm of his heartbeat. She breathed in so deeply, so fully, that she shuddered. How was he always so calm?

When they finally pulled apart, she looked into the face she'd missed so much. "I'm sorry for what I did to you," she said. "For what I did to us. I've been wanting to say that for so long."

An emotional shade closed over his eyes. "Not now, okay?" he said.

She sensed that he was holding back, that if things had been different, he would have kissed her hard, right there in the old hallway. The heat of his body, the flash in his eye, the sigh that escaped all spoke loudly what he worked so hard to suppress: his desire for her was still there. If only the bridge back to each other wasn't broken.

"You're right. This is not about me," she said. "This is about Brownie. I just need you to know that I made a mistake, and I hate myself for it."

"Emma, please."

She stepped away. Once again, she'd taken him from warm and open to cold and closed. She chastised herself as he moved toward the front door. "I was just about to go to the hospital," she said. "Is that okay?"

"They won't let you in to see him. You're not family." The compassion in his voice had completely disappeared.

"Right. Do you want me to take the flag down for him tonight? I'm right here. It's no problem."

"No," he said, walking out her front door. "That's my job now."

She couldn't imagine how she must seem to him—a desperate, red-faced, regret-filled, liar of an ex. One he used love but clearly no longer did.

"Bye, Emma," he said.

He shut the door tight before she could reply.

"Bye, Scruggs."

Chapter Twelve

I T WAS PAST noon when a blonde figure in the same gym-sculpted shape of her mother came strolling up the old wooden walkway from the beach. Emma saw her from the kitchen window while mashing bananas for a hummingbird cake. "Mother! I thought you'd left!" She ran out the back door to meet her.

"Do you think I have the first clue how to summon one of those Ubie-car people? I am stuck here whether I like it or not." She brushed the sand off her feet and marched into the kitchen, assessing the dirty dishes in the sink.

The woman was exasperating. "I can drive you anywhere you want to go," Emma said.

"And leave behind this mess? I think not." She had her usual pursed-mouth look of judgment that always made Emma feel like a terrible disappointment. "What are you making?"

"A hummingbird cake," Emma said. "So, you're really not gonna go back to Daddy?"

"Don't be silly." She washed the sand from her hands before moving on to the dirty dishes.

Emma folded flour into her mixture while trying to decide what her mother meant by that. What was she being silly about? "So you are going back?"

"I told him I'd come home before Christmas. Maybe by then he'll let you come, too."

"Yeah," Emma said. What was the purpose of leaving him if he knew she was coming back? Not to mention, if she'd been the mom, she would only agree to return if her daughter was invited, too. They should've been a mother/daughter package deal. Emma opened a can of crushed pineapple and poured it into the batter, knowing full well things would never change.

"Emma Shea," her mother began, "why on God's green earth are you baking a hummingbird cake? You know that neither of us needs the calories."

"I'm making it for Brownie's family. He's in the hospital."

"In the...*what*? We just saw him last night!"

"I think he had a stroke. I found him this morning when I saw that he hadn't left any apples."

"Oh my heavens." Clarissa stopped scrubbing and stared out at the beach. "I guess we all knew something like this would happen at his age." She went back to the dishes. "Make sure you don't forget to put the cinnamon in that cake."

"Yes, ma'am." Emma worked in silence until after the cake was in the oven. Then she set the timer and sat with her mother. "Mama? You know the guy that the news is talking about?"

The judgmental pursed-mouth look was back. "The one with the stupid name? I can't even bring myself to say it."

"Scruggs, Mama. His name is Scruggs."

"Who gives a human being a name like that?"

"Well, I'll tell you. His mother and father gave that name to him. And his mother is Brownie's daughter."

Clarissa dried her hands on a tea towel and threw it on the counter. "How many daughters does he have? There is no way that no-good cheat of a low-class man is in any way related to our Mr. Howell."

"He's his grandson." She wanted to add that Scruggs wasn't no-good or a cheat or low-class, but she couldn't win that battle—yet.

"You are wrong." Her mother paced the black-and-white floor of the kitchen, not angrily, but as if she'd simply been standing too long and needed to move. When she spoke again her voice was as sweet and smooth as honey butter. "I will talk with you about your love life all day long, but only if it involves my gorgeous son-in-law, Trent Broadway, do you understand?"

Emma had forty minutes until the cake was ready to pull out of the oven, and she wasn't about to spend it talking about Trent. "I'll be upstairs if you need me." She climbed the creaky stairs and turned right at the top, into the speakeasy. The room sparked her imagination so intensely that it didn't take long until every other thought was pushed aside. There was something magical about such a fancy place in the center of a dowdy old nailed-together green wood house.

She pulled out a cerulean-blue chair and sat staring at the shimmering golden sign over the bar: The Firefly Club. It was the perfect name for the hidden room in an overgrown home. An unexpected spark of light in the middle of the ordinary. She pulled out her phone to see if there was any historical information online. Even one old photo of the place in use would be incredible. She typed and scrolled and read and explored until she happened across a simple definition. *Firefly Girl: a young woman who adopts an unconventional behavior and look. Term largely used in the '20s to describe women who acted contrary to what was commonly expected by going out, drinking, smoking, dancing, wearing makeup, etc.*

"Mama!" Emma rushed down the stairs just as the cake alarm went off.

"My word! What is the emergency?"

"I had this thought last night—if upstairs is The Firefly Club, we should be the Firefly Girls. And Mama, look at this!" She showed her mother the definition. "I think this house is telling us who we're supposed to be."

"Drinking and smoking?" From the expression on her mother's face, Emma might as well have told her she was getting a face tattoo. "I don't think so."

"Not that part! Unconventional. That's what we need to

be. Why are we always trying so hard to follow the rules?" She typed in the word *unconventional.* "Look at the definition: *not based on or conforming to what is generally done or believed.* How will things ever change or get better if we always do what is expected of us?" She was so excited, she was practically vibrating. "Mama, we don't have to please everyone. We don't have to fit into some mold people from hundreds of years ago decided women were supposed to fit into."

"We have rules for a reason, Emma Shea. What do you want? Bedlam? A society filled with self-centered ne'er-do-wells? Do you believe we should no longer stop at red lights, too?"

"Mama, what I'm saying is—"

"Get that cake out of the oven before it burns."

Emma found a pair of hot pads and carefully placed the cake on the stovetop to cool. "I don't want to be a good little girl anymore, Mama. I married the wrong guy because I was trying to live up to everyone else's expectations. I want to do what is right for *me.*"

"So, you're going to become a harlot? You're going to go live under a bridge somewhere?"

"I'm not going back to Trent."

"Well, then. You will be starting off your new endeavor well…as a disappointment to everyone who loves you."

There was no use arguing. "You know what, Mama? Your great-grandmother was Frances Mackey, and that means you've got some Firefly Girl in you whether you want it there or not."

She hmmphed. "Don't ice that cake until it is completely cool."

"I won't."

"Good." Clarissa moved to the back porch, leaving the door wide open. "Have you seen an orange cat around here?"

"Yes," Emma yelled back. "Louie has been in several times."

"There's a heating pad in the bathroom cupboard. Leave it out for him if it gets cold."

"I will."

Emma's phone rang. The caller ID said Birdalee Mudge-Crane. "Hey, Birdie!" she answered.

"Now listen," Birdie said. "I am doin' me a video, and I need whatever it is you're cooking for Brownie."

"How do you know I'm cooking something for Brownie?"

"Oh, please. We all are. What is it?"

"A hummingbird cake."

"Excellent. Now, I need you to bring it over to Tea and Tennyson before you deliver it to the family. I am teaching a lesson on hospital manners. Can you be here by two o'clock?"

Emma checked her watch. If she put the cake in the refrigerator to cool, she could probably make it. "Sure."

"I might have a representative from the family there as

well. Ya get what I'm saying? Can you see me winking over the phone?"

"You mean Scruggs?"

"Yes. So look pretty."

The thought of getting frozen out by Scruggs again, especially when all she wanted to do was help and commiserate, felt overwhelming. She'd just recovered from being so close to him, from needing and anticipating something that felt like an almost but had proven to be a never. And at Tea and Tennyson again? That place brought back so many memories, so many feelings, and they all centered around Scruggs loving her.

Birdie was telling her to gussy up for more pain, and that wasn't the easiest thing to do considering she still hadn't picked up any of her own casual clothes. She wasn't about to wear a dress and heels to the coffee shop. She said goodbye to Birdie and hung up.

"Mama, I've got to go shopping. Can you ice the cake?"

"Shopping for what?"

"An outfit."

"In Crickley Creek? Have you lost your mind? What are you going to buy, a flour sack?"

"I only brought my good stuff, and I don't have time to drive to Beaufort. What do you suggest I do?"

"If you had half a mind, you'd wear something from this house."

"Everything here is from generations ago, and I need to

look good."

"First of all, there are vintage treasures in these drawers that Coco Chanel herself would be proud to wear. And second, *why* do you need to look good? You won't give your own husband a chance, and now you're going to see some other man? Is that what you're doing?"

"It's not like that."

"Don't fool yourself, Emma Shea. It is exactly like that."

What had felt like a whirlwind of need quelled to a light breeze. "Oh my God, Mama. You're right."

"It is not healthy to go from one man to the next, you understand? You chose one, and now you've got to stick with him."

"But I chose the wrong one."

"I refuse to believe that."

"Mama. He chose the wrong one, too."

Still, her mother had a point. She shouldn't set her heart on Scruggs. She had penance to pay. She deserved to be lonely right now. Emma texted Birdie. *"I'm so sorry I can't help with your video today. Something has come up."*

Birdie texted back. *"Fine."* Which was strange, because Birdie never gave up without a fight.

Chapter Thirteen

EMMA WAS DRESSED in a sleeveless black mock-turtleneck and black-and-white checked shorts her mother found for her in the downstairs dresser. She was barefoot in the kitchen, which was an enormous breach of etiquette, but did it matter if no one else was around? Clarissa had taken her car to the Piggly Wiggly for bran cereal, Chardonnay, and a sympathy card. Emma swirled the last bit of the cream cheese frosting onto the cake.

She nearly stuck the knife through the dessert when the front doorbell rang. Mama probably needed help with the groceries. She licked the frosting off her fingers and ran to answer it without opening the tiny door first.

"Since you won't come to me, I will come to you." Birdie held her cell phone up high and sideways, recording. "Where is the cake?"

Emma led her to the kitchen, grateful she'd gotten dressed but worried that Birdie would catch her bare feet on the video. "I found the recipe in a tin from one of my grandmothers," Emma said.

"And why did you choose a sweet dish rather than a casserole?"

"Well, dessert has a way of making people feel better. At least for a second." Emma wasn't sure whether she should look at the camera or the woman behind it.

"And would you ever consider merely sending a card?"

"Well, I suppose it depends on how well I know the person."

"And how well do you know Mr. Howell?"

"He's my neighbor."

Birdie turned the camera around to herself. "Now, this show is about manners and not about current events, but when opportunity strikes—" She turned the phone back to Emma. "Y'all might recognize this woman if you're from these parts. All y'all out there in Australia and, you know, Indiana, won't know her from Adam, but trust me when I say she has gotten herself in a little marital pickle."

Emma turned her back to Birdie's camera and pretended to ice the cake.

"Her husband is Trent Broadway. I'll insert a little photo for you here. But she's in love with Brownie Howell's grandson. His name is Scruggs, and I'll add his photo, too." She paused. "Ain't that just a *thing*? The slickster or the nerd—which one will she choose? And will that person choose her back? I reckon we should all pay attention because this is about to work itself out one way or another. Emma will be cuddled up by the fire for Christmas with one of them."

Emma fumed as she made curlicues with the knife. She had half a mind to stab it straight into Birdie's black heart. How dare she do that to her. As soon as Birdie shut off her damn phone, Emma would rip her head off.

"Any comment, Mrs. Broadway?"

Emma put on her sweetest smile. "Thank you for your concern, Birdalee. This may come as a surprise to you, but I have feelings. Just like you and just like everyone else. And all of this hurts. A lot. If you want to teach about manners, maybe now would be a good time to practice an apology. My life is no one's business but my own." She picked up a handful of chopped pecans and sprinkled them onto the top of the cake.

"Ooh, and she's got some sass, too, ladies and gentlemen."

"Birdie. If you post this anywhere, so help me I will chop off your head and ship it to China."

"Like I said folks—sass."

Emma reached for Birdie's phone despite the fact that her hands were covered in pecan dust. "Oop!" Birdie backed up so quickly, she ran into the kitchen table. "Hey! You best not injure me now. I know you're upset, but I'm on your side."

"You are not on my side, Birdie."

"You can't blame me for trying to please my fans."

"Birdie! If you want to show my cake, then fine. But if you post anything else, I'll—"

"You'll what? Send my head to China?"

Both women turned when a figure darkened the hallway. "Y'all okay in here?"

"Scruggs!" they said simultaneously before launching into loud, overlapping explanations of their positions, growing more insistent with each word.

Scruggs whistled to shut them up. "Hey! Both of you, pipe down."

They did as they were told, mainly because the whistle was so high-pitched and shrill that they didn't want to suffer it again.

"Give me your phone, Birdie," he said.

She handed it to him like a child. He watched the entire video, then deleted it.

"My fans will never forgive you," Birdie said.

"Did you not hear what she said? She has feelings, Birdie. And this is not all her fault."

Birdie held up a plump finger with a long red nail. "I wasn't placing blame, Mr. Scrumptious."

"You shouldn't be."

Emma was stunned. "It is my fault," she said quietly. "Everything is my fault."

"Well, according to my granddaddy, we do better when we know better."

Her mouth dropped. Had he just provided her with an excuse? That she didn't know better than to marry Trent? She wasn't sure how to feel about that. She wasn't stupid, and she didn't want to be made to look that way. But had he forgiven her? Did she even deserve to be forgiven? She was a stew of emotions, her head spinning with hope and questions.

Birdie held her phone upright on the table, pretending not to be recording. Scruggs grabbed it from her before she could react and stuck it in his back pocket.

"Y'all take things way too seriously," Birdie said. "It's all in good fun."

"Make fun of yourself, Birdalee. Not other people," he reprimanded her.

"Oh hush, Scooby. Don't go ruining my day."

Scruggs shot her a look.

"How's Brownie?" Emma asked.

"Granddaddy's doing okay," he said. "The mouth of the South over here said you had something for him. She asked me to stop by."

It was Emma's turn to shoot Birdie a look.

The woman shrugged innocently.

"Yes, I made him a cake," Emma said. "Well, it's for your family or whoever wants it, really." She pointed to the pecan-covered cake on the counter.

"That looks good enough to sell at a store," he said. "I'll be next door until he's out of the hospital, so I'll take it over there and make sure he gets a piece."

Emma tried not to look happy about that.

"What about your place?" Birdie asked.

"There's nothing about my house that needs me every day, and Waffles gets all riled up about the beach. She might love it more than I do."

"You have a house now?" Emma asked.

He nodded. "A ranch-style near the marina." It was almost a whisper. "With a three-car garage, a dock, and a boat slip."

"Wow. That's really great." She was happy for him, even if that meant his future wife and kids would enjoy that house instead of her. The man deserved every good thing he got.

Birdie was clearly getting bored. "All right, you two. I have work to do, and if I can't get any content made here, then I am boutta make like a baby and head out." She put her hand out to Scruggs, and he placed her phone on her upturned palm.

"Bye, Birdie," he said to her back, as she strutted away.

"Bye, y'all," Birdie said, adding, "and sorry, Emma."

"It's okay," Emma said. An apology from Birdie was like receiving a dog turd wrapped up in a bow. But none of that mattered. She was now alone with Scruggs. Her heart pitter-pattered like Louie's claws on the tile floor.

Scruggs didn't seem to notice. He was just as steady as he always was. "You know," he said, "my grandfather really likes you."

"I really like him, too." She tried to control the jitter in her voice.

There was a long pause before Scruggs said, "Alright,

then. It's time for me to go."

"Let me get you the cake." She grabbed the plastic wrap from a drawer and went to work draping it carefully over the top and tucking it under the plate.

"Hey, Emma?"

She carefully brought her eyes to his.

"What is it that you want?" he asked.

You.

But that was only part of the truth. "I want to fix a mistake." There was more, though. There was something deeper, something she hadn't even thought to herself yet. "To be honest, I'm still figuring it out. But I know I don't want to be the person I have been raised to be. I want to be happy with myself, whoever that person is."

"Now, I really can't speak for Emma Shea Broadway," he said, moving toward her in that self-assured way that always made her toes tingle. "I don't know her. But maybe you ought to start with Emma Smith. That girl was pretty great."

She handed him the cake. "Turns out she was a cheater and a liar."

"She also worked hard. She was funny, and she cared about people. Waffles really loved her, and everybody knows that Waffles is a great judge of character."

Emma led him to the front door. "She really loved Waffles, too." Her voice cracked and she stood awkwardly with the cake between them like a spongy round metaphor. She'd put that impediment there, and now he was stuck holding it.

"Um," he began, "do you think you could open the door for me?"

She quickly pulled it open. But he still couldn't walk through. Coming down the overgrown flagstone path was her mother, and she didn't look happy.

"Hello, Mrs. Abernathy," Scruggs said.

"Do not speak to me," she said. "You are a disgrace."

"Yes, ma'am." He attempted to walk past her.

"Mother!" Emma yelled. "Be nice!"

"You thought you could seduce my daughter?" She stood like an angry child with her head tilted backward so her mad face was aimed directly at him. "Don't try to tell me you didn't know who she was."

"Mama!" Emma placed herself between her mother and Scruggs, both stuck on a walkway surrounded by overgrown plants.

"You don't remember me, do you?" he said calmly.

"I have never known a person with a name like yours. Never."

"How about Marshall?" he asked.

Her face fell.

"My middle name is Marshall, and that's what my mother's side of the family calls me. You used to call me that, too. You've known me my whole life, Mrs. Abernathy. I'm just all grown up now."

With her hand covering her mouth and her eyes as wide open as the front door, she moved out of the way for him to pass.

"Thanks for the cake," he said.

Chapter Fourteen

"OH LORD." CLARISSA Abernathy fanned herself. "Oh good heavens." She had trouble catching her breath. "His mama and daddy are divorced. That's why I didn't recognize the Willingham name. She's been remarried since that boy was a toddler. Their surname is Coleman. I have been under the impression that his name was Marshall Coleman all these years." She shook her head like she was trying to expel the name like water from a dog. "I cannot believe I did not recognize him. His mother never called him Scruggs. Not once. I swear it."

"It's okay, Mama." Emma helped her inside and fixed her a glass of filtered water.

Clarissa leaned against the wall like it was a full-body crutch. "I mean, a name like Scruggs Marshall Willingham is just a triumph of bad taste."

"Why is this even bothering you?"

Mrs. Abernathy took a small sip of the water. "His mother was one of those superficial-type friends years ago. You know, the kind that you have for a season and then allow to fade away?"

"Oh." Emma had a feeling she understood now. "So she didn't like you? Or does she know something you'd rather her not?"

"Trust me when I say that you had better wipe that satisfied look off your face or I will wipe it off for you."

"None of this is satisfying, Mama."

"Go to the car and get me my wine before I have myself a fit."

When Emma returned, her mother was sitting at the kitchen table, still stricken.

"His mother"—she bit her mauve-painted lips together—"is wealthier than we are."

"What?"

"That man she married when Marshall was little? Mr. Coleman? Well, he is the owner and—" She squished up her whole face, then attempted a deep breath that fell short. "He has a technology business."

Emma was afraid her mother might have a panic attack. There was a distinct look of terror on her face.

"He is quite well-known." Clarissa waved for Emma to hurry up with opening the wine. "The man owns a private jet airplane."

Emma finally managed to pull out the cork and pour her mother a hefty glass of Chardonnay.

"Oh thank God." Clarissa took a large draught. "Why are you not more upset?"

"Upset about what?" Emma asked.

"That you should've married Scruggs Willingham!"

"Because his stepfather has money? Have you lost your mind?"

"Well, who do you think is going to provide for you? Santa Claus?"

"What are you talking about, Mama? I have a trust coming in just a few years."

"Well, maybe you ought not count on that."

"Don't count on the trust?"

Clarissa looked around the room before she lowered her voice. "It's possible that your daddy has made some bad investments."

"Wait." Emma grabbed a glass and poured a quarter of the contents of the wine bottle into it. "So this is why you pawned me off on Trent? Because there's no money for me?"

"That might be an extreme version of the truth."

"But still the truth."

Her mother shrugged and took another large gulp of wine. Emma hadn't touched hers yet.

"Your father is going to be so upset," her mother said. "I was supposed to keep you away from Scruggs, and now, now—I don't know what!"

"Supposed to keep me away from Scruggs?"

"Well, I am not here for my health."

"You said you left Daddy. That you saw me at the house in Beaufort and served him one last bourbon."

"You know I believe strongly in doing or saying whatever

is necessary to achieve my goals."

"Mama." Emma sighed like her mother was the child and she was the adult. "Which parts did you lie about?"

"Well, I did serve him his bourbon, but we both saw you at the house." She drained the glass of wine and then tapped on the rim to ask for another.

Emma retrieved the bottle from the refrigerator and gave her another healthy pour. If liquoring up her mother was what had to be done in order to get the truth out of her, then so be it.

"Your father, your husband, and I decided that I would move in with you in order to keep you away from Scruggs or Marshall or whoever he is. Gall-dangit."

"Daddy and Trent? You all decided?" Emma had to say it out loud in order to believe it. "So, you didn't really leave Daddy. And you were never really afraid that Daddy was going to come find you."

Clarissa snickered. "You acted like he was going to barge in here and fillet us both. When has that man ever laid a hand on you?"

"It's not his hands that scare me—it's his mouth."

"Well, you've simply got to let those words go now, don't you?"

It was Emma's turn to roll her eyes. "Mama? What does Scruggs's mama know that you don't want her to?"

"Oh, nothing, really. She just knew that every time I came to this house, something was up with me and your daddy. And our disagreements are nobody's business but ours. I mean, it is downright *embarrassing*."

"According to Brownie, you're not the first in our line with an unhappy marriage."

"Who said I have an unhappy marriage? I just need to get away from him every now and then. That's why your grandmothers left us this house, as a getaway. I happen to have a very happy marriage. You should know that."

A happy marriage? In all fairness, they did seem to be cut from the same cloth. Maybe the screaming and disagreeing was fun for them. And it was true that despite his bad temper, her daddy had never physically harmed either one of them. A fantastic thought hit Emma and she clapped her hands together. "Well, it looks like you are free to leave now, Mama."

"Yes, I suppose I am." She raised her glass as if to clink a cheers. "It's a win-win situation no matter which man you end up with."

"For your information, I don't plan to end up with either of them."

"Don't be stupid, Emma Shea."

"Not only does Scruggs have a girlfriend, but I plan to get a divorce and then *not* get married again for a very, very long time. Maybe forever."

"You're only saying that to wound me."

"Am I not enough for you, Mama? I don't need that trust money. I can stand on my own two feet with my nursing job. Plus, I help people. Does that mean anything to you?"

"Well, of course. It's just that we raised you for much bigger and better things."

"Do you need help packing?" Emma turned and walked into the guest room, noticing for the first time that a suitcase was hidden under the bed. When had her mother snuck that in there? "Want me to call you an Uber?"

"I'll just text your father. He'll come get me."

"Well, I won't be here when he arrives. Goodbye, Mama." She grabbed her keys from the bowl on the hallway table.

"I could kick you out of this place, you know," her mother announced to Emma's retreating back. "It's not yours yet."

The thought struck fear in her. The little house had been growing on her. And who would put the heating pad out for the cat? A cold front was supposed to be moving in at Christmas.

Her mother laughed again. "You look like a stiff little french fry. And I mean that in the best possible way, of course." She took hold of the bottle and poured more wine. "I'll let you stay. I'm not an ogre."

"Thank you."

"But only on one condition: either you get engaged to Scruggs or you make up with Trent. By Christmas."

"That's impossible. Christmas is a week away."

"The press must be fed. We need some good photos and some good news to provide them."

"Getting engaged to Scruggs is suddenly good news?"

"Well, not for poor Trent, bless his heart. But we could spin it real good."

"Do you even care about me at all, Mama?"

"Everything I do is for you, darling."

Emma shot her a look of disgust.

"I'm serious," her mother said. "You best find yourself another place to stay by Christmas Day unless you meet my terms." She drank the entire glass of wine she'd just refilled. "I'm only doing this because I love you, of course."

Emma slammed the front door when she left. It was enough that she wasn't getting the trust money she'd counted on her whole life, but now her mother was going to kick her out on Christmas Day? What kind of controlling, selfish, materialistic and, and…evil people were they?

She slammed the door of her car and nearly spun out trying to reverse out of the sandy, grassy driveway. She made it to the end of Blue Ghost Lane before realizing she had no place to go. She couldn't stomach running into Birdie or Scruggs, so Tea and Tennyson was not an option. The only errand she needed to do was to shop for clothes, but she barely had any money, thanks to Trent. What she really needed to do was to pick up her own clothes. It occurred to her that if her daddy was on his way to get her mama, she wouldn't run into him in Beaufort. That suddenly made it a great time to do the drive. Pulling out her phone, she texted Trent.

"You home?"

He sent a thumbs-up emoji.

"I'm on my way over. Can we talk?"

He sent another thumbs-up emoji.

Good. It was time to get to work on her plan—especially if she now had a deadline. She'd hoped to have Abby there to help her pitch their idea, but like the old cliché said, desperate times called for desperate measures.

She practiced her speech the whole way there, trying to anticipate Trent's reaction and find ways to redirect him to her point of view. Her biggest selling point was that he didn't have to get back together with her in order to save his reputation. He could have Abby. By the time she pulled up to the big marble stairs, she was ready.

Trent waited for her on one of the rockers on the front porch, moving slowly back and forth with a scowl like a father who'd caught his daughter sneaking out. She almost lost her nerve. When she reached the top step, he said, "I know what you're going to say. I already spoke with Abby. It's not going to work."

"She's perfect, Trent."

"She's damaged."

"Mental health issues are not looked down upon like they used to be. Depression is common and, thank God, there isn't much of a stigma anymore. This is a real opportunity."

"Opportunity? Screw you, Emma Shea." He stood, sending the chair into the wall with the force. "You're my wife. You understand? You're it, whether we like it or not."

Emma looked around to make sure no one was hiding somewhere and recording them. "Let's go inside, okay?"

He led the way into the old drawing room she had decorated with deep green velvet wingback chairs and coral-red ginger jar accents. It wasn't her best work. She should have gone with the bird motif in taupe.

"Listen," he began. "This thing is too far gone with the press. The only answer. The *only one*, Emma Shea, is for you to come back home. We have got to put this behind us and look like a happy little family. We should talk about having kids soon, too. If you're pregnant, they'll for sure think we're happy."

Emma had to sit for that one. "Pregnant?"

He looked as sure of himself as a professional wrestler.

"But we're not happy, Trent. We should absolutely not become parents."

"You have to admit, Emma Shea, we'd have some awfully cute kids."

He was turning on the charm, but it wasn't going to work. "You should've married Abby. You wanted to marry her. She told me. So what we need to do is become a united front. We both made mistakes, but we're going to fix them together."

"You're saying we should parade Abby in front of the press?" He threw his hands in the air. "Oops! I should've married this one instead. Silly me." He ran his fingers through his gelled hair, then wiped his hand on his pants. "You are insane."

"If we're both happy, what does it matter? If we're up-front about it, they'll have nothing else to talk about. We'll kill the gossip with honesty. Plus, that way, you can be with her."

"Why are you trying to pass me off to her, huh? You want that other guy?"

"No. I don't want that other guy. He is happy with someone else. What I want is to be happy with *me*, with the person that *I* am."

"Right." He laughed. "The only thing that will make you happy is a big house and plenty of do-re-mi. Is this not enough for you?" He waved his arm around the room. "Is this multimillion-dollar historic house on the water not enough?"

The truth was, it wasn't. There was a time when she believed that all she needed was the big house, the big ring, the luxury car, and designer wardrobe in order to be happy. But not anymore. She'd rather have five hundred dollars in her bank account and like who she was than live a lie in a mansion with Trent. She wanted to lash out at him for being so rude. To yell at him that she'd changed—and that she'd been orchestrating that change for a long time. "I need to get my things." She stood and walked to the grand staircase.

"We're not done talking about this, Emma Shea."

She took the carved mahogany steps to the second floor. It was strange to be back in their bedroom. She'd play-acted a part here, tried to convince herself that she had everything she'd ever wanted. So many nights she'd snuggled up to Trent, willing Scruggs out of her mind, forcing herself to feel something, anything, for the man in bed next to her. Some days were easier than others. But the nights were always difficult.

Her walk-in closet was exactly as she left it, filled with designer shoes and purses. She didn't want any of them. What she wanted were her old leggings, jeans, T-shirts, and sweatshirts—the ones she'd worn in college when she was just another face in the crowd and life was simpler.

She met Trent at the bottom of the stairs with a bag of her things. His normally slicked-back hair fell into his eyes, and he picked at his thumbnail. "You can do whatever you want with the rest of that stuff," she said.

She'd definitely caught him off guard with that one. "You're not taking your handbags?"

"Donate them."

"Goddamn it, Emma Shea!" He stomped his foot like a little boy. "This is not funny. You have to come back here."

"I'm not laughing, Trent. We both made a mistake, and the way I see it, the only way to fix it is by being honest— together."

"I will buy you a Tesla if you come back by Christmas."

Emma put down her bag and took his long sweaty hands in hers. "Thank you for everything you've already given me, Trent. I mean that. Thank you." Then she picked up her bag and made her way out the front door.

"What do you *want*?" he yelled after her.

She threw her bag on the passenger seat and ran around to the other side. What she wanted was to get back to the little green beach house and find that her mother was no longer there. And she wanted Brownie to be okay. That was pretty much it for the moment.

Chapter Fifteen

AFTER THE BRIDGE from Charleston, the road to Crickley Creek ran for miles, eventually running straight through the downtown historic district. Emma was on autopilot, thinking about what she should have said, what she meant to say, and what she'd hidden from Trent. Nothing had been resolved, and since there was no way on God's green earth that she was going back to him, she had exactly one week to figure out where she was going to live. Not only that, but if Brownie was still in the hospital, she'd be spending Christmas Eve alone.

It was coming up on rush hour, so the traffic was beginning to get heavy. She reached for her cell phone to see if anyone had sent a message, telling herself she wouldn't read it while driving; she just wanted to see if one was there. Maybe something from her mother or news about Brownie. She grabbed the sparkly gold phone from the passenger seat next to her bag of clothes and when she looked back up at the road, a black object was dead ahead. There was no time or room to swerve. Emma stepped on the brake, gripped the wheel, squeezed her eyes closed, and braced for impact.

The crash sounded like metal hitting metal and felt like she'd run over a toolbox or the lid to someone's old backyard grill. The good news was that her car was still on the road and she'd made it past the object without her air bags deploying, but something up front was scraping along the road and sending up sparks. She pulled over and sat in the car until she stopped shaking enough to stand. Then she carefully checked for traffic and got out to check the damage. The front bumper portion of her car had been split in half and was hanging underneath the chassis. She didn't recall anything hitting underneath, and since she drove an SUV, maybe it was high enough off the ground to have not been damaged. But she couldn't be sure.

There didn't appear to be anything leaking, and her tires were still full of air—for the moment. Normally, she would call her daddy or Trent. They would know what to do, after they berated her for being so stupid. They would be right, too. She was stupid, and every person who passed by knew it. Anyone else would have seen the object, slowed down, and driven around it.

But she'd been reaching for her cell phone. Angrily, she wiped away the tears she hadn't meant to allow. Angry tears came easier when the person you were mad at was yourself, and that was a fact. She dug in her purse until she found a tissue and dabbed at the wetness to try and preserve her makeup as much as possible. It was time to act like an adult and call a tow truck, so she walked away from the road and into the weeds surrounding an old Civil War cemetery where she stood and called the first number she found. The tow truck would arrive in two hours.

She could hitchhike. She could call someone. Or she could walk to Tea and Tennyson. It was probably no more than a couple of miles from where she was stranded. It was almost four o'clock, and they'd be closing soon. Even so, someone who knew her would probably be there to shut the place down. At the very least, Krista's mother, Junie, would be working. Junie would surely let her hang out for a while, especially if Emma offered to help mop the floors and do the closing chores.

She pulled her tennis shoes from the bag on the seat and slipped them on with a pair of socks. Then she locked everything up and took off on foot in the direction she wished she was driving. Every honk from a passing car was like a lesson in humility. What must people think of her? That she had no one to help her?

Her whole body burned with embarrassment, so she tried to hold her mouth in a pleasant half smile so no one could tell. Christmas miracles were for television heroines. She couldn't even drive without hitting a large object in the road. The corners of her mouth began tilting down, so she pulled them back up. She should have taken the Tesla. She should have sold her designer purses. She really could end up at a homeless shelter on December twenty fifth.

With her face set agreeably, she walked casually but with

purpose. She *meant* to be walking along the side of the road in vintage non-exercise attire and a large designer purse. She did not wish for help or attention from anyone, she was just taking a lovely little stroll on a warm winter's day.

The problem was, she'd been so focused on appearing casual that she forgot to hurry. When she finally got to Tea and Tennyson, it was past four thirty, and the store was locked up tight. She knocked on the glass front door in case Junie was still there. When no one answered, she moved to the bench in front. The sun would be going down soon, and it would start to get cold. Where was everybody? It was like the downtown had been deserted. Was it a bank holiday? More than anything, she wanted to get back to the little house on the beach. It might not have central heat, but it was the warmest place she'd ever been. She jumped when the bell of the coffee shop door jingled.

"Emma?"

It was Scruggs, a pad of graph paper in one hand and the door to the store in the other.

"Oh, hey," she said. "You working on the day spa?"

"Yup. They've torn it down to the studs up there. The fun part is just now starting."

Emma smiled. It was strange to see him working in any capacity other than barista.

His face had questions written all over it. He'd never been good at hiding what he was thinking. "You, uh, need anything?" he asked.

"Just a place to sit for about an hour. And maybe a ride to my car. I'm waiting for a tow truck."

"For that fancy car of yours? What happened?"

She nodded. "There was something metal in the road."

He stepped aside and gestured for her to come in. "Might as well pass the time with some good music." He led the way up the back stairs to what Emma had known as Krista's loft, although Charlotte owned the whole building. It was sad to see the furniture gone and the space no longer a happy, homey haven. But the more Scruggs explained the plan, the more it sounded fabulous. A place of rest and retreat for everyone, with massage and facial rooms, a sauna, locker rooms, and a lounge. Crickley Creek could use a place like that. Scruggs had designed the whole thing, and he seemed so proud of himself that she wanted to take his hands and jump up and down, saying, *Can you believe it? Look how far you've come!*

Instead, she gave him a little clap and said, "It's really great."

The same crooked smile that used to take over his face when he had a big idea appeared. "Hold up. I'll be right back."

The tape measure on his tool belt rattled as he ran to turn on a little Bluetooth speaker he had set up. Scruggs had always been a sucker for music of all time periods and genres. Seconds later, a song from Tim McGraw projected through the empty space, bouncing off every piece of wood framing.

She recognized it as "Highway Don't Care," and judging from his face, it was supposed to be funny. A little kind-hearted ribbing to add some brevity. She laughed along with him when the lyrics were about driving too fast and trying to stay awake.

But what he'd clearly forgotten, and what hit her harder than the metal object in the road was that the song was about missing someone, about not wanting to live without that person. Tim McGraw's baritone felt like Scruggs was singing that he cared. Emma's stomach dropped to her knees.

The feelings she'd been suppressing for Scruggs had to be written all over her face. Music had a way of hijacking her emotions. It always had. With merely a few short lines, it grabbed her by the throat, reached in, and pulled out her heart.

He fumbled with his phone to pause the song.

"I'm so sorry," he said. He used the sleeve of his wrinkly flannel shirt to wipe at the wetness she didn't even realize was on her face. Their eyes locked together like they'd both been lost until that moment. Then he leaned in and slowly kissed her. "I do care, Emma. I do." He kissed her again.

"I missed you so much," she whispered into his lips.

As soon as she spoke, he pulled away. "I've got to close up shop," he said, making his way around the space and flipping switches like he was choosing willpower over desire. "I'll drive you to your vehicle."

"Okay," she said. She'd ruined the moment again. Every

time she tried to apologize or treat him like she used to, he shut down. "Thank you."

She followed him down the stairs. Was he berating himself for kissing her when he had a girlfriend? Knowing Scruggs, he most certainly was. She wondered for the gazillionth time who his unknown, unseen girlfriend was. Birdie didn't even have any information about her. Not that it mattered. He was taken, and that was it.

The tool belt around his waist wiggled as he walked, and she noted his body, although taller, was the same as a year ago. He had wide shoulders and narrow hips, the toned physique of good genes and an active lifestyle. If he ever lifted weights, it was done in his garage rather than a gym, so that he could load and unload a truck or carry his beloved across a threshold. Trent, on the other hand, worked out at the most popular Beaufort gym in order to make business contacts and to look good in a suit.

She put her fingers to her lips where Scruggs's had just been.

When they were both in his truck, which he'd parked around back, she said, "I promise I won't say anything about what just happened."

He had his arm across the seat, reversing out of the parking space. He cut his eyes to her, then back to the road. "Good."

His truck was clean and warm, and after parking behind her broken-down Mercedes, he was nice enough to stay with her until the tow truck showed up. They barely said two words, unless they were about Brownie, who was still clinging to life after what Scruggs called a hemorrhagic stroke. She didn't have the guts to tell him Brownie had invited her over for Christmas Eve with his family. If Brownie made it out of the hospital in time, then she would give Scruggs a heads-up. Especially if he was planning to bring his girlfriend.

Her stomach sank at the thought as she watched him make notes on his pad of paper, some sort of to-do list. There was no music playing, which was rare for him, but after that last song, they might both be too sensitive. The only sound was of cars whizzing past and heat gently blowing from the vents. She looked out the window at the old cemetery and tried to read the names. EZEKIEL PORCHER, DIED 1928, AGE THIRTY-THREE. EASTER NELSON, DIED 1909. It was hard to read the ancient, cracking, overgrown tombstones. She turned back to Scruggs. Here they were, the luckiest people in the world, still young and living their lives. They had everything. *Everything.* That old gumption in her belly started stirring. Ezekiel. Easter. She said a silent prayer for them both. *God, bless them. Tell them someone down here is thinking of them.*

"Scruggs," she began, "I have to tell you something." She took a deep breath, and the fire in her belly flared with what she was about to say. "Your grandfather invited me over for Christmas Eve, and if he is at home, I plan to come. If your girlfriend is there, I promise I will not stay long and I will be very nice. Also, I know you don't like to hear it, but I really am sorry about how everything happened. I have made my bed, and I will lie in it. I am not going back to Trent, and I can't stay in my mama's beach house past Christmas, so I will be applying for jobs somewhere and finding myself an apartment. I might not see you again after that, so I need you to hear my apology now."

He almost never looked angry, but from his squint and the way he bit his lips together, he was clearly frustrated. "And how is it going to help me to hear your apology?"

"We only have one life to live, so when I mess up, I want to make it right."

"That's still about you, Emma. Everything you just said is about you."

"Well, I want you to have the satisfaction of knowing I regret what I did."

"And I'm supposed to feel better? Because you regret breaking my heart?"

"Yes. I wish I hadn't done it."

"Yeah, well, me too. But that doesn't put it back together, does it?"

Emma looked at him, her mouth hanging open. "You're not normally like this."

"You really hurt me, Emma." He put his pad of paper on the console as if to say, *if we're doing this, then I'm all in*. His voice grew louder. "I thought you were the one. I had our whole future laid out, and then one day you just up and disappear. I didn't even know if you were okay. You wouldn't answer my texts or calls. Then I hear that you married some other guy? That your name wasn't even Emma Smith?"

She nodded. "I deserve that."

"Do you? Is that what you deserve, Emma? One minute you're strutting along with your designer bag and your fancy car, coming from some place I don't care to know about, and the next minute you're saving my granddaddy and baking us a cake. I don't know what to make of you." He ran his fingers through his hair, his brow furrowed. "And I shouldn't have kissed you just now. All it did was bring those danged feelings back. I'm not ready for you to be here. You shouldn't be back in town."

The sound of tires on gravel grabbed their attention. The tow truck was pulling up behind them.

"I understand," she said. "I thought you'd just forget about me. That it wouldn't hurt you because you are so steady and stable. You deserved so much better."

"I should hate you," he said.

She opened her door and climbed down. "And I understand if you do. Thank you for the company. And for the ride."

"You're welcome," he said, putting the truck into gear. He paused, then put it back in Park. "I'll just wait here to make sure the tow truck gets you squared away."

"And I won't go to Christmas Eve. I'll just drop off some goodies for Brownie. I'm sorry I said that."

There was no hint of a smile when he said, "Shut that door, it's getting cold in here."

Despite the fact that he was upset with her, it was the first time in a long time that the pit of regret in her stomach didn't feel quite as hopelessly deep. It had felt terrible, but at least he'd finally listened to her. At least he'd gotten a little anger out.

"See you next door," she said to his departing truck, more grateful than ever for Frannie's little beach house.

Chapter Sixteen

WHEN EMMA AWOKE the next morning, she was strangely happier than she'd been in a long time. She put on the blue bathrobe and got the coffee brewing. Then, on a whim, she checked the front porch. There, on the little table by the door, was an apple. She gasped and ran outside to get a good view of Brownie's house. The flag was up and flying. "Yay!" she said aloud, clapping. Grabbing the apple, she ran back to the kitchen where she'd left her phone and called Scruggs.

He answered immediately. "Is Brownie home?" she asked. "He left me an apple!"

"Oh shoot. No, Emma. He's not. That was me. I did it for him."

"Oh. Did he ask you to?"

"I just knew that's what he'd want me to do."

"Oh," she said again, trying not to sound too disappointed. It was really sweet of Scruggs to fill in. "Are you going to see him today?"

"Yeah, I'm headed to the hospital now."

"Please give him my best. Tell him I miss him."

"I will."

"Okay, then." She hesitated. It was nice connecting with him on the phone, but she didn't want to push it by saying too much. "Have a good day."

"You, too."

The cat was on the back porch and for some reason, she was grateful for his fuzzy face. She opened the door. "Hey, Louie. Want to come in?"

He immediately looked away.

"Fine," she said. "I'll come out there with you, then." She took her mug of coffee and made herself comfortable on the rocker nearest the door.

Louie gave her the side-eye, checking her out without moving his head in her direction. When she ignored him, he suddenly became interested in her. Like a too-cool teenager, he casually walked to her chair and jumped onto her lap. She held her mug out of the way as he circled her lap three times before plopping himself into the shape of a cat donut. Never before had she experienced an animal so brazenly obnoxious and sweetly chummy in equal parts. She pet his head, and he let her.

An hour later, he lay lightly snoring, still in the same position on her upper thighs. Her coffee mug was empty, and she had resigned herself to being stuck on the chair until he woke up. There was no way she was going to disturb the moment, no matter how long it took. What did she have to do, anyway? Her car was in the shop, and she had no one to buy Christmas presents for, no reason to go anywhere. She might as well allow herself to be held hostage by a sleeping cat for the rest of the day.

With her head leaned back on the chair and her eyes closed, she tried to solve her list of problems. Could she get her money back from Trent without having to go through a lawyer? She needed it to pay the deposit and first month of rent somewhere. Did she want to go back to Beaufort? She could probably get a job any number of places. There was a hospital nearby in Charleston. Maybe she could move to Folly Beach. It was a lively place to be. But the traffic could be bad. Sullivan's Island, maybe? It was quieter, as long as you didn't mind the huge cargo ships that passed so close to the beach.

The truth was, the place she loved the best, the place that sparked her imagination and held her heart, was tiny, unimposing, nothing-fancy, gossip-ridden Crickley Creek. She was falling in love with her great-great-grandmother, who'd first chosen it. And she was in love with her old patriotic next-door neighbor, who'd helped make it special. She was also in love with a certain architect—a nerdy one, with wrinkly shirts and a childhood Lego addiction that he'd carried into adulthood. She would ask him the next time she saw him if he still sat on his living room floor and put things together when he was stressed. Her heart hurt as she remembered the vase of Lego bricks that used to be in the shape of flowers. She couldn't ask him to remake them for her, but she sure missed them. They'd been the best flowers she'd ever gotten—colorful and rot-proof.

But even those hadn't lasted.

Her hand made its way to the cat's back, and she petted and scratched as he slept. "What am I gonna do, Louie?"

"You're gonna stay right here."

Emma's eyes flew open at the sound of a man's voice, and she nearly dumped the cat from her lap as she sprang up.

In the chair next to her was Brownie.

"Brownie!" She reached over and he took her hand in his. "You're home!"

His face was grumpy, as always, but his eyes had a light to them—a happy, knowing twinkle. "You have to take care of the roots in order to heal the tree."

"What?"

"It's the Gullah proverb written on that tray of your grandmother's."

"Oh!" she said.

"You aren't ready to leave here," he said.

"I don't want to go."

"Listen carefully." He gave her hand a little squeeze.

Emma leaned in, appreciating his warm, fleshy, perfectly solid mitt.

"You have to give something up in order to become your true self." He said each word slowly, like they really mattered.

"I do? What is it?"

"That's for you to figure out. But I can tell you this, you are on your way."

The cat was awake and watching Brownie cautiously. Emma finally noticed that Brownie was wearing a suit—a light blue seersucker one, and his wavy white hair was deeply parted and freshly combed.

"Are you going somewhere? You look great!"

"I'm going to see my best girl." His face relaxed into a winsome state, like he'd been waiting a long time for this, his eyes red-rimmed and watery with excitement. "Don't give up on my grandson."

"Well, I think that is more up to him at his point."

The corners of his mouth lowered. "Hear what I say."

"Okay, let me get this straight." She let go of his hand and put up her fingers in succession. "One, heal the roots. Two, don't leave. Three, figure out what I have to give up. Four, make sure the thing I give up is not Scruggs."

"Good girl. Yes. And, five, turn on the lights." He chuckled. "The first one and the last one are from your grandmother Frannie."

Emma repeated with a smile, "Heal the roots, and turn on the lights."

The cat was sitting up now and staring at Brownie like he was soaking in every word. "I'm so glad you're back," Emma began. "I was really getting worried."

Brownie stood. "Don't worry about me," he said, taking the back stairs slowly and carefully. "I'm as happy as a child on Christmas morning." He did a little jig, then shuffled his way next door, stopping at the edge of the property to turn back to her for a moment. "And, Emma? On Christmas Day, you need to believe it."

"Believe what?"

"You'll know."

The cat jumped off her lap and followed Brownie. What a great morning it was turning out to be. Brownie was back. He could talk and walk, and he even knew she wasn't Frannie. She felt as light as the air on that cool, sunny day. It was time for a shower, then she would make a Christmas gift for Brownie. Maybe an oyster tree? She could collect bleached-out oyster shells from the spot near the jetty down the beach and glue them onto a conical frame. It would be a small one, a tabletop version like the one upstairs, with a star made from a dried white finger starfish, if she was lucky enough to find one. Suddenly, her day looked busy. The best kind of busy.

Emma spent three hours beachcombing, and as she approached her house with a bag full of oyster shells, she noticed a figure sitting on the beach. She increased her pace, hoping it was Brownie out trying to catch another shark. She recognized his hat, his old ice chest, and his bright red fishing pole. When she realized the figure in the hat was Scruggs, she jogged a little faster.

"Hey!" she called out as she approached.

He reached up an arm to wave.

"I'm so happy about Brownie! He came by this morning. What a relief!"

Scruggs looked at her strangely. His eyes were puffy, his nose red. "Granddaddy died this morning," he said.

A violent shudder wracked her entire body. "What? No! I just saw him. We had a whole conversation." She dropped her bag and plopped down next to Scruggs, trying to make sense of what she'd experienced. "He gave me a list. He told me what to do. He—"

"He's gone, Emma."

She shook her head. How could that be? "This is impossible." She'd held his hand! It was warm!

Scruggs put down the fishing pole and covered his face with his hands. She'd been so concerned about her other-worldly visit, she'd forgotten for a second that Scruggs had just lost a man he'd loved his entire life. She threw her arms around him, and he leaned his head onto her shoulder. "I'm so sorry, Scruggs. I'm so, so sorry."

After a few minutes, Scruggs pulled away and asked, "What did he say to you?"

"He said a lot. But the most important thing is that he's happy. He said he's as happy as a child on Christmas morning. And that he's going to see his best girl."

Scruggs produced a closed-mouth smile, and for a moment, his pain seemed to lessen. "My grandma." He nodded as it continued to sink in. "I'll tell Mama. She'll want to know that." A few seconds passed before he added, "You know what he used to do for me on Christmas morning? He'd put on his boots and step onto a pan of my grandma's flour. Then he'd leave Santa's footprints going from our fireplace to the tree. It was always the most magical part of Christmas for me. I believed in Santa until I was fourteen because of that man. He had a way of making everything special." He chuckled. "Of course, if you accused him of being the one to do it, you'd get yourself in trouble."

They sat in silence with the infinite waves of the Atlantic before them and the homes of their ancestors behind them. Her thoughts were consumed with Brownie, and it looked like his were, too. If someone had come walking by, they would have thought they were newlyweds, or at least old friends. They had a connection—one that was bigger than their circumstances, bigger than lies that had been told so often that they somehow became truth. Bigger than mistakes.

She glanced at his profile, stifling the desire to hold his hand. There was an ease and a purpose to their bond, and now she understood why. It was because it had existed long before they had.

Chapter Seventeen

"I DECLARE," BIRDIE said, the bulbs of the appliquéd Christmas tree on her red sweatshirt swaying, "if I have to deal with one more tacky person this Christmas, so help me I will castrate every man on this planet and put an end to the human race."

Emma knew better than to show up at Tea and Tennyson at Birdie's behest. Absolutely nothing good could come of it. But boredom had a way of winning over common sense, and there she was, along with Krista, a very pregnant Charlotte, Virginia Buchanan, and about ten members of the Junior League.

"If I have to go to the Piggly Wiggly to purchase ingredients for one more funeral casserole, I'm gonna keel over and die," Birdie said. "Now, put all y'all's casseroles on the table while I get to filming. Did anybody here make brownies?" She laughed at her own stupid joke, but no one else did. "You know, cause we're here for *Brownie*." She waited for laughter, but all she got was exasperated smirks. "Y'all are no fun."

Emma didn't think Birdie was funny at all, but there was

definitely something hilarious about all of the cakes and casseroles covering the table. If the pan wasn't disposable, and most of them weren't, every person had a method of marking which one was theirs. The last name of half the families in Crickley were represented on the dishes in variations of Sharpie marker, printed labels, and even a professionally personalized dish proclaiming a BOWEN FAMILY RECIPE. The names were both a method for getting the glassware returned and a ploy for making sure it was known by all that the family had fulfilled their meal-providing duty.

The Styrofoam boxes from Virginia Buchanan were the only ones that had come straight from a fancy restaurant in Charleston. "I couldn't bother Middie to do any more cooking today," she said, "what with all the prep for my holiday supper. I'm certain Brownie's family won't mind a meal from a very expensive establishment instead." Each of her vowels were so drawn out, the sentences seemed to take forever.

Birdie rolled her eyes. "Alright, y'all. This is part two of my casserole series. I need to interview each one of you about what you made." Instantly, several arms were raised. "What is it?" Birdie asked with loud annoyance.

"We're gonna miss the funeral if we don't hurry this up," said a woman in a bright Lily Pulitzer winter dress.

"I believe we have less than twenty minutes," piped in another woman, who was more sensibly dressed in black.

"Oh for heaven's sake," Birdie said. "I guess that's what I get for trying to be sensitive to the family by doing this here." She flapped around the table in frustration. "Here's what we're gonna do. When I call your name, you will point to your casserole and yell out what it is. Okay? Can y'all handle that? Then we'll all have ourselves an old-fashioned procession to the church."

The room full of women nodded in unison. "Let me set my phone to record." She put her phone on a tripod, made sure the entire group could be seen, then pushed the red button. Birdalee Mudge-Crane was a force of nature without a camera present, and she was a category five hurricane in front of it. The woman practically grew three sizes.

"Welcome to my fans," she said into the camera, "and to any newbies out there who might just now be discovering me. Go ahead and hit those Like and Follow buttons now. You don't want to miss a second. Now, let me first point out my special guests."

Emma cringed. Of course. Birdie would never miss an opportunity to call a person out.

"We have the very famous Krista Hassell. Go ahead and follow her, too. She's got just a few million more fans than me, but I'm about to change that!"

Krista waved at the camera.

"What'd you cook, Krista?"

"I made pickled shrimp." She obediently pointed to the dish she'd brought.

"Nice," Birdie said. "Next, we have Virginia Buchanan, of the very wealthy and esteemed Buchanan family. She used to live on Katu Island out here by Crickley but now finds herself in Charleston. Ginny? What is your offering?"

Virginia put on her most gracious smile and stepped forward. "I am far too busy to cook these days, so I am providing the family and their funeral guests with a lovely selection of dishes from none other than Magnolias restaurant in Charleston."

"How kind," Birdie said, as Virginia remained stiffly smiling at the camera, pointing at a large bag of Styrofoam. "Next, we have our tainted princess, Emma Shea Broadway. I'm certain y'all recognize her."

Emma smiled half-heartedly.

"And what did you bring for your ex-boyfriend's grand-father's funeral?" Birdie asked sweetly, then quickly covered her mouth. "Am I allowed to say that?"

"I made one of my grandmother's recipes," Emma said, ignoring her. "There was a note on her recipe card that said Brownie was particularly fond of it. It's a beef tenderloin." She pointed toward a beautiful covered tureen in red transferware. There wasn't even a name on it.

Emma heard Virginia gasp and turned to look in time to see a sour expression settle onto her face. Birdie continued on to every other woman and still managed to get them out the door on time. Emma caught up with her in the parking lot. "Is something wrong with bringing a beef tenderloin?" she asked.

Birdie chuckled. "Are you referring to Virginia's reaction? Oh, I do hope we can see it on the video. You just stepped on her toes is all. She was making up for the fact that her dish was not homemade by overspending. Then you showed up with an expensive dish, and it was your grandmother's recipe, too. You know as well as I do that you won the competition."

"I wasn't trying to compete."

Birdie was too busy manhandling her ever-popular hash brown casserole to care. "Of course you weren't."

Emma caught a ride with Birdie to the funeral. It was a nice production, and there was plenty of delicious food in the church basement afterward, but the whole thing was excruciating. Too many eyes kept going back and forth from her to Scruggs. He seemed to understand as well as she did the importance of keeping their distance. There was just one moment in the basement when everyone had a Dixie plate filled with food and Emma happened to walk past him and his mother. He literally reached out and pulled her over. "This is her, Mother. This is Emma."

Emma had a mouthful of green bean casserole and was embarrassed that her plate was loaded almost beyond capacity. She'd even put a large piece of pound cake on top in case it was gone when she went back. She quickly looked around for a place to put down the plate and found a random chair in a corner that could hold it. Then she ran back to Scruggs and his mother.

"I'm so sorry about that," she said, extending her hand. "Hi."

"Marshall has told me a lot about you." His mother managed to say the words without malice, and instead of taking Emma's hand, she took her whole body into an embrace.

Emma winced both at the fact that they'd been talking about her and at the unexpected show of forgiveness. "I should probably take this opportunity to apologize to your family for all of the embarrassment I've caused," she said.

His mother shook her head, her eyes kind. "My daddy never suffered fools, and he pegged you as a good egg right off the bat. We all make mistakes, alright? It's learning from them that counts."

"Thank you." Emma could hardly believe what she was hearing. She'd thought his mother had been furious and didn't want to show her face because of the bad press about her son. "I'm also so sorry about your daddy. I only knew Brownie for a short time, but I really loved him."

Scruggs's mother took Emma's hand in hers. They were small and soft, like the rest of her. "Darling, don't you spend another second worrying about us, okay? And as far as my daddy goes, you said it yourself. He's happy now. I cannot tell you how much it means to me to know it."

"Yes, ma'am," Emma said. "As crazy as it seems, he really did tell me that."

"I believe he did. That is just like him."

Scruggs watched the exchange with an expression she couldn't read.

"I do intend to make things right again," Emma said. "You know, with my situation."

"Do what you need to do, sweet girl. Just don't expect everyone else to have the same definition of right." She patted Emma's hand. "And that's okay." Then she winked before her attention was overtaken by a guest coming over for a sympathetic hug.

"Yes, ma'am," Emma said. The woman was brilliant. An absolute saint. No wonder Scruggs was so wonderful. Whatever his intentions might have been when he pulled her over, it had been a gift to meet his mother.

THAT EVENING, EMMA wrapped a thick quilt around her shoulders. The cold front had moved in, and if she didn't get brave enough to light the little stove in the family room, she was going to be in for a miserable night. She wore two pairs of socks and a T-shirt and leggings underneath her sweatshirt and pants. Still, she was about as warm as a penguin. There was a stack of firewood by the fireplace in the downstairs bedroom, and she added that to what was beside the stove.

Her phone rang, and the sight of Trent's name made her even colder. "Hello?"

"Seriously, Emma Shea. What in the hell are you doing?"

"What are you talking about?"

"Do you ever look online? There are pictures of you walking down a busy street like a danged hobo. They are everywhere. People are saying you've lost your mind."

"Well, maybe I have." She sat on an old club chair next to the stack of wood, staring at her outdated surroundings.

"We have got to solidify a plan. *Now*. You are causing all kinds of damage to my campaign."

"Do you even care *why* I was walking down that road? If I'm actually okay?"

"Considering you answered the phone, my guess is that you're fine."

"I appreciate your concern."

"Cut the sass, Emma Shea. I need you at the house on Christmas Eve."

"I know. I've been thinking about it a lot, and if the press sees that we are getting along, that we're still friendly, it might help with getting them off our backs. You know, give them what they want in order to shut them up. I'll be there."

"Good. That way they can print the photos for a happy Christmas Day story. And make sure you wear something appropriate. Classy. And curl your hair."

"Fine." When had she ever not worn something classy and appropriate?

"You better not mess this up, hear me? I'll have the guest room made up for you."

"I'm not staying, Trent!"

"Of course you are. That is the whole purpose of you coming back."

"I am not going to live my life in a sham of a marriage where I'm sleeping in the guest room of my own house."

"Just stay until I'm elected governor."

Emma held the phone from her face like the device was crazy. "I'll be there for dinner on Christmas Eve, but that's it." She'd stay in a tent on the front lawn before she slept in the house with Trent again.

It no longer mattered that she was cold. Her anxiety and frustration were a huge distraction from her physical discomfort. She was climbing the stairs to the bedroom when her phone buzzed with a text.

"You have heat over there?" It was from Scruggs.

"No. Not yet." She would have heat, as soon as she lit the dusty, dangerous, antiquated potbellied stove.

There was no answer for several minutes. Then another text came through.

"I just put Granddaddy's space heater on your front porch."

She ran down the stairs and opened the door, hoping to catch a glimpse of him. A blast of cold wind hit her in the face. She squinted into it, but it was too late. He was gone. What she did find, however, was a big silver heater sitting like a quiet hero on her stoop. "Thank God," she said as she carried it inside. It was surprisingly light.

"Thank you so much! You saved my life." That text might

have been a little overly dramatic, but it sure felt like the truth right now.

"Save the wood for the stove in case there's a power outage."

That was disheartening. She thought she'd just successfully avoided that darned stove.

"You have water?" he asked.

"I'll fill the pitcher in the fridge."

"Fill up the bathtub, too. And leave the faucets dripping so the pipes don't freeze. You have food?"

"Yes."

"I'll stay next door just in case."

He was staying next door for her? *"Are you sure?"* she asked.

"They're calling for a mighty big storm."

"Thank you." She added a red heart emoji. There was so much more she wanted to say. She'd never known a man to do something so thoughtful. What was in it for him? Nothing except maybe the satisfaction of knowing he did something kind for someone. Maybe it meant that, eventually, they could be friends. Yes, there was definitely enough hope for that. She carried the heater upstairs, plugged it in, and aimed it toward the bed. It didn't take long before she was toasty warm under the covers. Her nightly friend, the moon, joined her through the big picture window, and thoughts of Scruggs hunkered down next door filled her with the most snuggly heat, the kind that came from feeling cared for.

If there'd been a camera in that room, she was certain she would have been seen smiling in her sleep. And that sleep was the deepest, most deliciously rejuvenating sleep she had ever experienced.

The next morning, there was an apple by her door, and the flag was up and flying. The rest of the house was freezing, so she took the little heater with her to the kitchen. She sautéed the apple in butter and brown sugar to top the oatmeal she had warming in a small saucepan while her coffee brewed in the pot. She had Trent's party tomorrow, and some big changes were coming. There was much to do to prepare.

Chapter Eighteen

THE HOT WATER heater in the old house must've been replaced recently because the showers were the best she'd ever had—strong water pressure and steamy, endless warmth. With no one around to be accountable to, Emma took a half-hour shower. She shaved her legs, deep conditioned her hair, and stood with her face in the water until her skin turned red and she had to turn away in order to take a deep breath.

With a towel wrapped around her body and one twisted into her hair, she rifled through her bag to find something warm to wear. The best she could do was a pair of jeans and an old College of Charleston sweatshirt. The bedroom was comfortable thanks to Brownie's space heater, but the rest of the house was like an ice castle. She layered a T-shirt on underneath and decided to wear her puffer jacket inside. The most important thing was to dry her hair before she left the room, or it might freeze right there on her head.

From the big window, the beach looked like a desolate, miserable planet, and she hoped the shorebirds had a sheltered place to go.

Louie! She'd forgotten to put out the heating pad. She ripped the towel from her hair. Poor Louie! Practically skiing down the stairs, she retrieved the heating pad from the guest room and opened the door to the back porch. There, at the bottom of the sandy stairs, was Louie hissing and swatting at Scruggs's little Yorkie as Waffles ran circles around the fluffed-up orange cat.

"I'm so sorry, Louie," she said as she plugged in the heating pad and set it underneath a blanket next to the house. "You can come inside the house, you know, but I'll leave this here just in case." She pointed to the warming station. "Come here, Waffles," she said, grabbing the little dog midstride. She pressed her lips into the soft furry face as the dog licked the air around her, straining to make contact. "I missed you so much," she said, accepting Waffles's copious kisses on her cheek. "But you have to leave Louie alone."

The cat didn't seem grateful at all. He just casually sashayed through the door she'd left open as if he hadn't just been in all-out fight mode. He even gave Emma a look like she was late to help him, a traitor, and not the person who rightfully belonged in that house. She deserved for him to tear up a couch or pee on a rug to spite her.

Scruggs came ambling around the corner, and Emma was horrifyingly aware of her freezing unbrushed hair and lack of makeup. "You staying warm enough?" he asked.

"Yes, thanks to the heater." She attempted to finger-comb her tangled hair with one hand while holding his dog with the other.

"Did you get the text?"

She hadn't looked at her phone for at least an hour. It was still upstairs in her bedroom. "What text?"

"Charlotte's at the hospital having her baby."

"No way! Now?" The baby wasn't due until New Year's Eve.

"Birdie's at the hospital already, getting into everybody's business. She's demanding that we all join her."

He had his hands in his pockets and his back turned to the wind. She gestured for him to come inside and carried Waffles into the kitchen. Her head was beginning to feel like a snow cone. "I'm not sure Charlotte is going to want an audience," she said. "Plus, she could labor for days." Emma had been taught not to insert herself where she wasn't wanted.

"I'm gonna stop by anyway," he said. "I've known Charlotte and Will for so long, they're like family to me."

Inexplicably, Louie, the world's grumpiest cat, was purring and rubbing on Emma's ankles. She squeezed Waffles to her chest to avoid an altercation. "I was planning to take an Uber to Charleston this afternoon to do some shopping," she said, planting another kiss on Waffles's head. "But if everyone is stopping by the hospital, maybe I will, too."

He reached for his dog and she reluctantly handed her over. "Can you be ready in twenty?"

"You mean, go with you?"

"Of course." He snapped his fingers at the cat at Emma's feet. "Want some grub, Louie?"

The cat's ears perked up, and he trotted behind Scruggs and Waffles without even a backward glance at Emma. Emma had better dry her hair fast. It was going to take every bit of that twenty minutes to fix herself up.

Exactly on time, she rang the doorbell at Brownie's house. Scruggs answered as he was putting on his winter coat, and seeing him coming out of Brownie's house was like witnessing Brownie himself as a young man. Scruggs was a good man, a steady, forgiving, thoughtful, loving human being who was not afraid to be who he was. When everyone else gave their girlfriends real flowers, he made them out of Legos. He'd rather stay in on a Friday night and watch Marvel movies instead of going to a bar or a fundraiser or a country club dinner, and when his grandfather was sick, he took over the man's self-imposed responsibilities. What man under thirty would willingly raise the American flag every morning and take it down every night? Plus, he'd left her an apple.

And this was the man whose heart she'd broken. How dare she do that to him.

His eyes kept moving to her, like he was trying to hide the fact that he appreciated how she looked. He apologized to Waffles for leaving, then locked the door. "That was fast!" he said to Emma.

"You said twenty minutes."

"Impressive." He laughed.

"Thanks," she said. He looked like a hot nuclear physicist dressed up as a lumberjack. "I like your plaid jacket."

The ride to Charleston was comfortable. They were like old friends with no need to fill the silences with small talk. "Looks like we'll have snow for Christmas," he said. "The weather's gone all cattywampus, but it's fine by me."

"I don't think I've seen snow since I was eight years old."

"Yeah. A lot of things have to go right. The ground has to be below forty degrees in order for the snow to form, and the upper atmosphere has to be around fourteen degrees for ice crystals. But there is a cold air mass about to collide with a warm, moist one, so we might get lucky."

She loved it when he explained things, even if she had no interest in the details.

"Listen," he said. "I'll keep staying next door in case we lose power. If you need me to, I can light that stove for you."

"I don't want you to have to do that."

"I want to."

"Thank you," she said, hoping he could hear the sincerity in her voice.

The hospital maternity ward was packed with people. "What on earth was going on nine months ago?" Scruggs asked, quickly doing the math and answering the question for himself. "March. Yep, that'd be spring. Ain't that just how nature works?"

Birdie was stationed in a corner, and either she or someone else had moved the waiting room chairs into a circle. "Hey, y'all! Come join the party." She motioned toward two empty chairs. Emma recognized Will's parents, his sisters, Virginia Buchanan and her son, Jackson. "Y'all just missed Krista and Johnny. They did a little drive-by baby check-in."

Emma and Scruggs took seats next to each other, and Virginia watched their every move with a capricious smirk on her face.

Birdie immediately pulled out her phone and held it in their faces. "Now," she said. "I am doing a segment about baby manners, and I need to ask y'all some questions. Scruggs. If Charlotte and Will's baby had a big green alien head, what would you say?"

His eyes grew wide. "What in the heck kind of a question is that?"

"Just answer it, Scooter-booter."

"Fine, Birdbutt. I would say what any decent person would say—congratulations on your baby."

Birdie nodded. "And what if the baby was just plain butt-ugly?"

"There is no way that Charlotte and Will would have an ugly baby."

"You never know," Birdie said. "And anyhoo, we're talking in general here. There are thousands of unsightly babies around these parts. I see them all the time."

Scruggs shook his head. "I believe the right thing to do is to just say congratulations."

Virginia spoke up. "People will know that you think the baby is unattractive if you don't say it is cute. You have to say it's cute."

Birdie swung the phone around as Virginia was speaking, then whipped it in to Emma's face. "Do you agree?" she asked.

"Well, I think every baby is cute, so that's easy for me."

"You cannot possibly think every baby is cute," Virginia said.

"Even if they look like a little old man or a rat?" Birdie asked.

"Yes! It's a brand-new baby!"

Birdie turned the phone to herself. "Baby manners rule number one: Always say the baby is cute, even if it's hideous. And rule number two, if the mama pushes that baby out fast, do not insinuate that her vagina is oversized."

Emma knew she would regret showing up at the hospital.

"Right, Emma?" Birdie said. "We wouldn't want to embarrass a brand-new mother in that way. A person must bite their tongue about that sort of thing, even if it is glaringly obvious."

Emma nodded. "I don't think that the amount of time a woman labors has anything to do with…what you said."

"I mean," Birdie began, "it's okay to ask questions in private, of course."

"About her lady parts?" Emma asked.

"Or you could just mind your own business," Scruggs

said.

"Isn't that what I just said?" Birdie swung the phone far too close to his nose. "Gossiping is a no-no."

Birdie stopped recording with a highly annoyed show of pushing the red button on her phone. "I can cut that part out when I edit the video."

"Y'all, tomorrow is Christmas Eve, and we're supposed to start getting snow." Allison Rushton, Will's mother, did her best to change the subject away from her daughter-in-law's private parts. "Can you believe it? Right here in the Lowcountry."

There was much chatter about the snow and plans for Christmas, which turned into asking who planned to remain at the hospital until the baby showed up, which led to Scruggs mentioning that he would be taking Emma home soon, which gave rise to questions about Emma's old house on the beach. When she shared that she'd discovered a secret room and that it was a genuine speakeasy, you'd have thought she'd just announced that Anne Frank was living in her attic. Every last person was riveted. They wanted to know every detail and pored over the pictures in her phone. She hadn't put much thought into it, but when they finally stood to leave, the words fell from Emma's mouth.

"I'm having an open house on Christmas Day. I'd love for you all to come by and see it. Bring whoever you want."

It felt right at the time, but as she crawled back into Scruggs's old truck, she kicked herself. Now she had less than forty-eight hours to pull off a party in a house that wasn't even hers. A house she was supposed to vacate on that very day, unless, of course, she got back together with Trent or engaged to Scruggs. Neither of which was going to happen.

Chapter Nineteen

DESPITE THE WIND and temperatures in the high thirties, Scruggs dropped Emma off on Broad Street in Charleston. She didn't ask him to, it just came about in conversation and he said he had things to do in Charleston, too.

It was strange to walk around the city alone knowing that Scruggs was somewhere waiting for her text. Thankfully, it only took two stores and four cold and cramped dressing room try-ons before she found the perfect demure dress for Trent's party. She was even able to track down some outdoor twinkle lights at the Walgreens by Marion Square. It was windy and colder than she'd ever felt in the Lowcountry before, but her puffer jacket was warm, and she wrapped her wool Burberry scarf around her head and face to keep the heat in.

She was more than ready to have her car back from the shop. It was uncomfortable to be reliant on other people for transportation. She texted Scruggs to pick her up. With her bags at her feet, she waited by the entrance to the Francis Marion Hotel. Across the street at the park, she watched a man cuddle under a filthy blanket next to a tree. There was nothing to cover his head, and it was only going to get colder that night. Surely, there was a warming center open somewhere, she hoped. When Scruggs's old Ford Bronco pulled up in front of her. Emma opened the door and said, "Just one second. I'll be right back." She ran across the street, unwinding the scarf from her neck as she went. "Sir?" she asked. "Would you like this?"

The man nodded, and she handed it to him.

"Thank you," he said. "Merry Christmas."

"Merry Christmas." She ran back to the car wishing she had done more but grateful that her parents weren't around so that she was free to do something, no matter how small. They would have been horrified that she spoke to him, and if she'd given him cash, she would never have heard the end of how she'd just perpetuated someone's drug problem, how she hadn't been helping him at all. She didn't know what the answer was, only that she was old enough to decide for herself if and when she would be generous.

"That was nice," Scruggs said.

Brownie's voice filled her head. *You have to give something up in order to become your true self.* She knew in that moment exactly what to give up...her raising. She would give up the crazy family beliefs, the me-before-you, and the everything-must-appear-perfect mentality that had been forced upon her since the day she was born. Her parents' values did not have to be her values. From this moment on, she was going to use her own intuition and trust that her internal guide was far better than living in fear of what other people might think.

When Scruggs pulled into the driveway on Blue Ghost Lane, Emma wanted more than anything to hole up in front of the space heater with him, watch a movie, and sip a cup of hot tea. Instead, he helped her bring in her bags from Piggly Wiggly, where they'd made a quick stop on the way home. Emma was on the verge of panic about having invited folks to a party with only a small number of hours to prepare, most of which should be spent sleeping. But by the time he said goodbye and walked out her back door to Brownie's house, she felt like she might be able to get it all done after all. She surveyed the kitchen full of food that needed to be prepped and cooked.

There was something she had to do first.

Grabbing one of her grandmother's old fuzzy hats from the closet, she zipped up her jacket and dragged a ladder from the carport to the big cinnamon crepe myrtle out front. *Turn on the lights*, Brownie had said. She hoped he'd been talking about these. With frozen fingers and a numb nose, she climbed to the top and there, stuck in the flesh of the tree, were the rusted remnants of lights that had adorned it once long ago. That was when she knew for sure. These were the lights she needed to turn on.

Brownie had said the message was from Frannie, so it was Frannie she thought of when she finished wrapping the small bulbs around the trunk and as high on the branches as the ladder would allow. When she plugged the extension cord into the house, the tree lit up like sunlight and starlight and fireflies and Christmas. "There you go, Grandma Frannie, with love from one of your Firefly Girls." Despite her frigid skin, she was compelled to stay outside, staring at her accomplishment. "Thank you," she whispered. *Thank you for this place, for your legacy, and for your strength.* And in that moment, she knew that no matter what happened in Beaufort tomorrow night, no matter where she had to move, or what sort of job she found, she would be okay alone. She could do it.

That night, Emma stayed up prepping the menu for the Christmas open house. She had recipe cards from an old tin spread out on the kitchen counter. The cream cookies from someone named Flossie Teegarden sounded divine. And the nitey-nites? They called for preheating the oven and then turning it off and leaving them in overnight. Perfect.

She cracked six eggs, separating the yolks, then prayed that her mother or one of her grandmothers had stocked the kitchen with an electric beater. So far, none of the women had let her down. In the bottom cabinet nearest the refrigerator, she found it. It was avocado green, and there was some rust at the top, but when she plugged it in, it worked. She whipped the egg whites into a froth and imagined her guests smiling as they tried her food. Birdie would probably ask for all of the recipes, and she would for sure, without a doubt, pull out her phone to take videos of the speakeasy.

It would be just like the raucous parties of the roaring twenties before the big stock market crash. Her friends would be eating and drinking and dancing and celebrating Christmas together. One of the best things about her party would be its lack of stuffiness—the magic of a hidden room that allowed her the freedom of not caring if the rest of the house was perfect. It might even be the beginning of regular open houses.

Wouldn't it be selfish of her to keep such a fabulous spot to herself? She could invite new friends as she made them and have theme parties where they all dressed for the era. She could even include a password—maybe *Frannie* or *lightning bug*—that people had to whisper before they entered. She could host baby showers and birthday parties. Her mind spun and her heart swelled with the beautiful fantasy. Carefully, she folded chocolate chips and walnut pieces into the meringue. Yes, this Christmas party was going to be the beginning of many epic get-togethers.

In her excitement, she momentarily forgot that she had hours of work to do. With a little luck, she wouldn't have to stay in Beaufort too long tomorrow, and she could spend most of Christmas Eve cleaning, decorating, and cooking. It was almost ten o'clock when she got a text from Scruggs.

"You still planning to join us for Christmas Eve supper to-morrow?"

She'd assumed that since Brownie had passed those plans

were now off. Staring at her phone, she tried to come up with a nice way of saying no, a way that didn't make Scruggs think that she was ditching him for Trent—again. She couldn't leave it to a text. She had to call him.

"Hey," she said when he answered. "I just saw your text."

"Mama made her world-famous ambrosia salad. Make sure you come hungry. We like to eat early, around noon."

"Scruggs. I'm so sorry. I thought that since your grand-daddy, um, isn't with us anymore, that I was no longer invited."

"Oh." The disappointment in his voice was clear. "Did you make other plans?"

Here we go. "Well, I thought your girlfriend might be there, and I didn't want to complicate things, so yes, I did."

"I don't have a girlfriend," he said flatly.

"What?"

"I just told you that to keep you away from me."

"Oh." Her heart pounded in her chest. He wasn't in love with someone else. He was single, available, his heart unencumbered. She could barely breathe. Did he have any idea how much that news affected her?

"Did you make plans with your folks?" he asked.

"I'm actually not sure if they'll be there." Her voice came out breathy and weak.

He was quiet for a few seconds. "But you're going back to Beaufort."

There it was. Just as soon as she felt like she might have a chance with him, it was all about to blow up again. Unless—she was thinking so quickly she hadn't yet put together all of the pieces—unless he went with her. Then he would see how it was between her and Trent. He would witness the mistake she'd made. He'd see firsthand that *he* was the one for her, not Trent. He'd be there to witness her plan. "I'd really love it if you could come with me," she blurted.

"To Beaufort?"

"If your party is at noon, maybe we can do both," she said. "Mine doesn't start until four."

"Am I getting this right? You're asking me to be your date? And where is this being held?"

"At my house."

"With your husband," he added.

"Yes."

There was a long pause. "Well, ain't that a thing." He laughed.

His reaction could have gone several different ways, and the fact that he was laughing felt like she'd just avoided a head-on collision.

"Do I need to bring my boxing gloves?" He laughed again.

"Maybe just some pepper spray." She laughed with him, but she was only half joking. Trent wasn't the violent sort—she would never put Scruggs in that situation if he was. But he was great at humiliation.

"Are you sure you know what you're doing?"

"I have a plan, and I know it's going to work. It's the perfect resolution to this whole mess."

"Tell you what. I'm gonna think about it, okay? For now, you just walk on over at noon tomorrow. And don't worry about bringing anything. We've got it covered."

"Thanks." It was okay that she didn't have an answer about Trent's party. It was probably better that Scruggs didn't go anyway.

With the addition of Scruggs's family supper, her day of Christmas Eve cooking had just been shortened to one brief morning. Even though she'd purchased the cheese straws and the shrimp cocktail rather than making them from scratch, she still needed to make artichoke dip, pimiento cheese, cucumber finger sandwiches, a charcuterie board, pulled pork in the Crock-Pot, and brownies topped with crushed candy cane icing. If she stayed up most of the night, she could do it.

Her phone buzzed with a text from Birdie a few minutes later. *"It's a boy!"*

There was instantaneous group text chatter. *"How's Charlotte?"*

"Will must be beside himself with joy."

"Is he cute?"

"Mother and baby are fine," Birdie wrote. *"He's got his daddy's ears."*

Emma had to laugh. Will Rushton was a great-looking guy, but his ears stuck out just a little.

"They named him Charles William. We're all calling him Charlie."

There was something about a baby being born at Christmastime that made Emma feel like the world might survive, and so might the human race. She took a moment to enjoy the relief, then dove back into the stress of creating a party with little time to prepare. She could see the light from Brownie's family room reflected on the sand from the window in her kitchen. Scruggs was probably watching a movie with Waffles, his laptop open to an architectural design program, tap-tap-tapping away at another design. The man had hundreds in his computer. Building things had been his stress reliever and dopamine inducer since he was a little boy with a bucket full of Lego blocks and a head full of ideas.

The thought of him alone next door made her grateful that she had too much to do in her kitchen. One glass of wine and she'd be knocking on his door.

Chapter Twenty

THE OCEAN BLENDED into the gray of the fog and the sky. It was a freezing cold day, and it looked like it. Emma had kept the electric oven on for heat while she was in the kitchen and an eye out for Louie all night. He never came to her door, and there was not a speck of orange fur on the heating pad. As if she didn't have enough to worry about this Christmas Eve, she was now sleep-deprived and highly concerned about a stray orange cat.

She opened the front door, and there on the table was a bright red apple. It was as hard as a golf ball, like it'd been in a freezer all night. As much as she enjoyed a cold, crisp apple, this one would need to thaw a little before she bit into it. She pulled her blue robe together in the front and saluted the flag. "Merry Christmas, Brownie," she whispered. "I'll have a bite of ambrosia for you." A swift, freezing wind blew her hair into her face, and she quickly shut the door.

Where on earth was the cat in that weather? If it didn't look like a creepy, foggy zombie movie set on Mars outside, she might take a little walk to look for him. Instead, she opened her back door and yelled his name. If she discovered a frozen solid cat in the next couple of days, she would never forgive herself.

She pulled the whipping cream from the refrigerator and soon, after adding powdered sugar and vanilla to the beaten mixture, she had sweet, fluffy whipped cream to spread on top of the yellow cake she'd made in a sheet pan the night before. She poked the spongy yellow dessert all over with a toothpick, poured an entire can of sweetened condensed milk over the top, spread the whipped cream and sprinkled coconut flakes. It was a foolproof and for-sure crowd pleaser—always moist and flavorful, and especially good with a strong cup of coffee. Scruggs had never tasted her cooking before, and she wanted to be sure he and his family would like it. He may have told her not to bring anything, but every Southerner knew those were merely words. You were always expected to bring something. And she, more than anyone, needed to make a good impression on his family. There was a lot to overcome.

By the time noon rolled around, the sun had made some progress in evaporating the fog, and the sky and ocean were blue again. But according to the weather reports, the break was going to be brief. Residents all over the eastern coast of the United States were being told to stay in on Christmas Day, that the roads would be icy and bridges would be dangerous. Snow was coming, and it was expected to stick. It was clear at the Piggly Wiggly the night before that everyone had heard the news—the shelves were empty of water, milk, and bread. Plus, there was a real dent in the beer and wine section.

Still, she'd managed to find a good bottle of Chardonnay. That would be the hostess gift for Scruggs's mother. She tied a red bow around the neck of it, covered her cake with tin foil, and put on her coat for the short walk next door. Her nerves were so on edge she couldn't feel her fingers or her feet. It was like she was floating above herself, watching like a butterfly as her hand raised to knock on the door.

Scruggs answered in a gray Christmas sweater covered in brown reindeer. He immediately took the bottle of wine from her hand and placed it on the ground outside where it couldn't be seen. "My stepfather is a recovering alcoholic," he said. "I should've told you."

"Oh! I'm so sorry! Should I run it back to my house real quick?"

"It's fine here." He moved from the doorway and placed his hand on the small of her back to usher her in. "Y'all!" he called out to God only knew how many members of his family. "Emma's here."

They walked to the back of the house, past the room where she'd found Brownie, and into the large two-island kitchen. At least ten people milled about, holding on to glasses of what Emma assumed was sweet tea or apple cider.

"Well, hey there, honey," said the pleasant woman she'd met at Brownie's funeral. The one with the same high cheekbones as Scruggs, the fluffiest blonde hair, and the sweetest disposition. "It's good to see you again," his mother said.

"It's so good to see you, too. Thank you for having me."

She held her hands out for the cake. "Did you bring us something?"

"Yes. I hope you like coconut. It's a—"

Emma didn't even get to finish her sentence before a girl close to her own age asked, "Are you trying to kill me?" She had her hands on her hips and stared at Emma like she was the Nightstalker come to murder her in her sleep.

"Oh my God," Emma said. "Are you allergic?" She hadn't even considered that possibility.

"Very," the girl said.

Emma shot a panicked look at Scruggs.

"It's my fault, Nikki," he said. "I didn't know or I would have told her."

The truth was, he had told Emma not to bring anything. And the other truth was even more horrifyingly clear: she shouldn't be here. She wasn't welcome. "I'm so, so sorry. I had no idea."

She grabbed the cake off the counter and hurriedly made her way back the way she'd come. "I'll be right back!" She tried to sound cheery, but it came out strangled as her throat clenched shut. She couldn't look at Scruggs; the humiliation was too great. She just opened the front door, grabbed the wine bottle from the ground, and ran as fast as she could next door.

Scruggs followed her, but she closed the front door before he arrived. He knocked and knocked, but she ignored it as she carried the cake and the wine up the stairs and set them on the bar in The Firefly Club. Shutting the mirrored door, she held her knees to her chest on the cerulean-blue curved couch in the far corner of the room.

Who did she think she was going to meet Scruggs's family after all she'd put him through? After all the media had put them through? Just because his mother was nice to her and he seemed to be on the way to forgiving her didn't mean the rest of the family had. Certainly, his cousin Nikki hadn't. She squeezed her knees and tried to squelch the tears that threatened to erupt. It wasn't going to get better, either.

Her entire day now felt off-kilter. She'd been so sure about Scruggs, and so certain about her plan that evening with Trent. But she no longer felt like she could pull it off. She hadn't even made it two minutes with Scruggs's family before she crashed and burned. The whole day was going to be a disaster—the party at Trent's was risky enough without the addition of this new crisis.

She heard the back door jiggle and a loud knock. *Go away. I have plans to drink too much wine and eat cake.* There was another jiggle, and her breath caught when she heard the telltale squeak of the old door hinges. Someone had gotten inside.

"Emma?" Scruggs called through the house.

Dammit.

CHRISTMAS IN CRICKLEY CREEK

"Emma, honey?" It was his mother's voice.

She hid her head in her knees. It was bad enough that Scruggs knew how to break into her house, but he'd brought his mother. That was taking the situation from a five to a thousand.

Unless she really wanted to be a child about it, she had to answer. "I'm upstairs," she said, wiping her face, hoping to minimize any black smears of mascara by rubbing them with her knuckles. She was still wiping when Scruggs and his mother walked in.

"I never knew this was here!" she said.

Emma faked a smile. "Isn't it great?"

Scruggs went straight to her while his mother took in the room bit by bit. "Hey," he said. "I'm so sorry about all that. No one's mad at you, I promise."

"I shouldn't have run off," Emma said as his mother approached. "I was up too late cooking last night, and there's a bunch of stuff going on in my life right now. I'm so sorry for making a scene."

"Honey." His mother sat beside her as Emma uncurled her legs. "It is Nikki's fault. She exhibited some very bad manners, and I apologize on her behalf. Listen"—she patted Emma on the knee—"can I tell you a little story?"

Emma nodded.

"My daddy, who you met, does not like ambrosia. But for years I thought he did, so I always made it for him. He would ooh and aah about how good it was, and he'd even take seconds, bless him, when all along the consistency of gelatin, the little wet marshmallows, and even the fruit made the poor man want to gag." She laughed. "I tell you this because, just like you, I made something I thought he would like. I was trying to do a good thing. And do you know what happened? Now, it's one of our favorite jokes, and the family would never forgive me if I didn't bring the ambrosia."

Scruggs nodded and smiled.

"The rest of us would very much like to try a piece of that coconut cake. And don't mind Nikki. She's not allergic—she just doesn't like it is all. In all honesty, she believes she has a bone to pick with you, but that's just because she's young and doesn't understand. You don't owe her a thing, and that includes an explanation."

Emma nodded. The tears had stopped running, but her nose hadn't. Scruggs hopped up and ran to the yellow bathroom, returning with a handful of tissues.

"I'm so embarrassed," she said.

"We are the ones who should be embarrassed. And, as much as I love my niece, I can tell you that this is not the first time Nikki has caused us some regrets." She stood and straightened her gold-and-black brocade pencil skirt. "Marshall and I will go now so that you can fix yourself up, but we expect to see you next door in—how long? Fifteen minutes?"

It was still strange to hear Scruggs referred to by his middle name. Emma nodded.

"I will grab the cake on the way out," his mother said, then added, "You know, you should make coconut cake your new Christmas Eve tradition."

As soon as the words came out of her mouth, Emma knew that was exactly what she'd do.

"Your mother kept this duct-taped underneath the rocking chair." Scruggs showed her a key. "I'll put it back for you."

Maybe if Emma had gotten more sleep, maybe if she weren't about to ambush Trent at his party, maybe if she didn't want to fix things with Scruggs so badly, she could have kept herself together. Instead, she had to completely redo her eye makeup three times. Every time she saw Nikki's face in her memory, new tears ruined what she'd just done. It took channeling Crazy Frannie, recommitting to her plan that night with Trent and Abby, and a promise to herself that she would tell Scruggs the whole truth, before she was able to stop the tears. It was more than fifteen minutes later, but she finally made it back next door.

When she walked in, everybody had a plate of a half-eaten piece of coconut cake, and the raves about how delicious it was didn't stop. At first it was uncomfortable, but the cake really was good, and the family was awfully nice for trying so hard to smooth things over. Almost every cousin and aunt and uncle treated Emma like part of the family. She was even served a heaping helping of ambrosia salad complete with Cool Whip and mini fruit marshmallows. After clicking spoons with Scruggs and his mother, they all dove in. "You just never know what your legacy will be, do you?" his mother remarked.

The only one who stood empty-handed was Nikki. She ate neither the coconut cake nor the ambrosia, and she made it crystal clear that she had the same amount of fondness for Emma that she had for the desserts. The sour look never left her face.

After three hours of getting to know his family, Emma couldn't wait any longer for an answer from Scruggs about the party in Beaufort. She crossed her fingers behind her back for good luck, walked him into the den away from the crowd, then asked him if he planned to go with her.

"I've been thinking about it," he said with a flake of coconut stuck to his chin.

Emma reached up and removed it for him.

He rubbed the spot she'd just touched. "I know you're gonna need a ride there, and I have waited until the last minute…"

"Oh," Emma said, "so you're dying to go. Great! Should be fun."

"About as much fun as you're having with my cousin Nikki. Maybe more, if Terrible Trent is as bad as he looks online." He chuckled. "But I guess I owe you now."

"That's right, you do. You owe me big. Like, *hang out with my soon-to-be-ex-husband* big. I mean, I ate ambrosia for you."

"You ate ambrosia for Brownie."

"True." She paused. Scruggs had been gracious to invite her to his family celebration, and he was being gracious by agreeing to go to hers. "Seriously, though. You don't have to go."

"I don't shy away from things, Emma. And I'm not afraid of Trent Broadway or any of the deranged news folk that might be there."

She took a deep breath and said a little prayer. "I have to tell you, Abby and I are going to tell the truth. Trent doesn't want us to, but we're going to stand together, as friends, and tell everyone that Trent should have married her. Marrying me was a mistake, but it's not too late to set things straight."

"Y'all are saying that against his wishes?"

"He thinks that the only way to fix things is to stick with the marriage and immediately start a family."

"Oh." Scruggs shook his head. "Yeah, that plan won't work."

The two made eye contact and held it a beat longer than a flash.

"But mine will," she said. "I know it. I—"

Scruggs cut her off. "I look good in this sweater," he said, smiling down at the dancing brown reindeer knitted into the gray yarn. "It'd be a shame to waste it on my family."

"So, you're going?"

"I wouldn't miss it for fifty pounds of shrimp and a ski boat."

Emma and Scruggs said their goodbyes. They had to get on the road if they were going to make it on time.

"Hey," Emma said as they excused themselves. She was excited to feel genuine affection for everyone in the room, except one. "I'm having an open house tomorrow if any of y'all want to come by."

"Will there be coconut cake?" one of the uncles teased.

"Only if Nikki comes," Emma teased back. The room fell silent, and she knew she was in trouble. It was too soon for sarcasm.

Nikki looked like she'd just been punched in the nose. "How dare you say that."

"Nikki," Scruggs began. "It was a joke."

Nikki bowed up at Emma. "I cannot believe you have the nerve to so much as speak to my family after what you did to Marshall. How do you think it feels to see your cousin made to look like a slimeball all over your Instagram feed? And all he did was care about you."

Scruggs moved in front of Emma, acting as a barricade. "None of that is any of your business, Nikki."

Nikki looked around the room at all of the stunned faces, and seemed to decide that she was speaking for all of them. "After what she did to Trent Broadway? You bring her to our family supper, Marshall? At Christmas? We should not be associating with someone like her." She leaned way over and pointed a long, white nail straight at Emma. "You are a toxic bitch."

"Don't believe everything you read," Emma said, pulling her shoulders back.

"You'd better shut your mouth, Nikki." Scruggs raised his voice. "You are the one being a bitch. You don't even know her."

"Look at what she's done to you! You've lost business! She destroyed your reputation!" Nikki yelled back.

"Business will come back," he said, shifting toward calm and logic. "And this is Crickley Creek, Nikki. Everyone here knows me. My reputation, just like everybody else's, is gonna change according to whatever people feel like talking about next week, and the week after that. It doesn't matter."

Scruggs's mother swooped in and ushered them toward the door. "Now you two be safe driving on those roads, they're going to get icier as the night wears on." She opened the door and dropped her voice. "I'm so sorry. We'll see you tomorrow at the open house, Emma."

"Maybe it'd be best if Nikki doesn't come," Emma whispered back.

"Don't you worry about a thing." She winked.

Scruggs grabbed her hand and pulled her toward his truck. The good news was, he had decided to go with her. The bad news was, if the next party was anything like this last one, Emma would have to move to Australia.

Chapter Twenty-One

HER HOUSE LOOKED like a painting. The rain that'd been on and off all day left the swags of magnolia leaves that ran along the front railing shiny and fresh. Even the large red bows dotting the leaves around the casing of the front door shone like new in the dusk. An enormous white-lighted Christmas tree was visible inside on the left, and wreaths adorned all of the upstairs windows. It was her own house, yet she felt as nervous and intimidated as a middle schooler in a high school hallway.

"You sure about this?" Scruggs asked as he followed her up the stairs.

She stopped and turned to him. "It will work. It has to work." She took another stair and turned again. "As long as you drive me home at the end of the night, it'll all be okay. And, I will leave with you at any time. You just say the word."

He nodded. "I can't believe I'm doing this."

"I can't believe you are either." Together, they walked to the front door. She lifted her hand to knock, then lowered it to use the handle instead. They stepped onto the polished heart pine floors and walked past the grand staircase toward the lively mumble of voices. "There she is!" Trent exclaimed when she entered the dining room. Everyone turned to look, their smiles wide and expectant.

"Hi," she said as Scruggs entered the room behind her.

Trent's face shifted from fake glee to genuine fury. The rest of the room went silent, presumably with shock. In the corner, next to the antique china hutch filled with Limoge, was her mother. She had the pinched face look of judgment that always stunned Emma's heart like a Taser, rendering it painfully numb.

Emma felt nothing. She was taking a chance, making a stand, one her family might never forgive her for—and she felt nothing.

Trent grabbed Emma by the arm and pulled her into the guest bathroom. His nostrils flared as he gritted his teeth and squeezed her bicep too hard. "What in the hell is he doing here?"

It was easy to pretend to be calm and sure. "He's part of the plan."

He raised a finger to her face. "How in your little peanut of a brain did you think it was okay to do this without my permission? This is my career you're destroying."

He walked the perimeter of the small room like a caged tiger while Emma stayed as close to the door as she could. She stole a glimpse at her phone. "Just be nice," she said. "Act like you and Scruggs are friends."

"That's your answer to everything, isn't it? Just be nice. Well, nice guys finish last, Emma Shea. And you are the weakest, stupidest, sorriest excuse for a wife that I've ever met. I cannot believe I married you."

"Exactly. But there's a girl who loves you. A girl who has done tons of work on herself and has learned and practiced so many emotional skills that she's nowhere near weak or stupid."

"Don't bring Abby into this."

"I'm not bringing her into this. I brought her *to* this." Emma pushed open the bathroom door and walked out. "She's at the front door."

Pulling her shoulders back like she was completely in charge of the situation, Emma marched to the front of the house. She wasn't just acting confident for Abby and Scruggs. She knew her plan would work. The press wasn't as rogue and savvy as people thought. Trent followed behind like a sheriff on her tail.

When she opened the door to Abby, she was overcome with optimism. Just like they'd discussed, Abby wore her blonde hair in a straight cut medium-length bob, a classy cream-colored dress, and pearls. She looked like a winter bride. With Emma's red hair and dark green velvet dress, they couldn't have been more different. Emma took her hand and welcomed her in while Trent stared at both women with pure undiminished panic.

Abby gently took his hand. "Don't worry. None of us

will have to hide anymore after this. We're giving the press the truth."

"It's not going to work," he said.

"If you're going to be governor, you will not spend your entire career trying to cover up a lie. I agreed that you should marry Emma because I thought that was best for you. But I was wrong. A lie is never best."

Emma tried not to smile as she witnessed Trent visibly soften. Abby spoke to him as if she was the authority, and he listened. In some ways it was highly amusing, but it also reminded her of why she thought the plan would work. Abby was impressive. She was genuine and relatable, and she was tough. If the press could see through her past difficulties, she could be the perfect person for the job. And for Trent.

Scruggs took Emma's hand and squeezed it, clearly recognizing the same thing. Trent was relaxing into someone else. His constantly clenched jaw, his darting eyes, all eased when he looked at Abby. Strangely, Emma didn't feel the slightest twinge of jealousy.

Two by two, led by Emma and Scruggs, the couples walked into the party. Judging from the open mouths and wide eyes of the guests, a person would have thought Elvis was alive and in the building. Two members of the local press were there as guests, and both made no effort to hide the fact that they were taking photos—not just of the couples but of the guests' reactions.

Emma's father had a scowl on his face that could freeze

the sun, while her mother was as expressionless as a porcelain doll. Emma touched Abby on the arm, and she turned around and smiled. "No matter what happens after this," Emma whispered, "you and I will always be friends."

"You got that right," Abby said, dropping Trent's hand in order to hug Emma. "I'm so glad we went to coffee that day."

As if following the girls' lead, Trent turned to Scruggs. "Can I get you a beer?" There were servers walking around with glasses of champagne, but Emma recognized Trent's question as an olive branch, an overture of friendship, and felt more pleasant toward him in that moment than she had in the past year.

"Sure," Scruggs said.

"You want anything?" Trent asked Abby and Emma.

They both shook their heads. With Trent gone, the three of them formed a social circle. "If y'all pull this off, it will be a Christmas miracle." Scruggs laughed as if he'd just cracked a joke, and both women followed suit.

Emma was acutely aware of her father staring daggers at her. When he made a move in her direction, she froze. Every instinct told her to grab Scruggs and flee, but she couldn't peel her eyes off of her father. He tapped Scruggs on the shoulder like a mafia boss deigning to interact with an associate.

"If you are not out of this house in three seconds, you will regret it for the rest of your life," he said in a tone so low no one more than three feet away could hear it.

"Daddy!" Emma spat the word, fear engulfing her like fire. "You don't know what you're doing. You're going to ruin everything."

"If one more word comes out of your hussy mouth, I will close it permanently," he replied.

Trent entered the room holding two beers. He assessed the situation quickly. "Mr. Abernathy, everything is under control here."

"This is your wife!" he yelled, grabbing Emma by the shoulders. "Do you see her? You promised to take care of her. This is a dereliction of duty."

The reporters in the room actively recorded the scene.

Trent carefully turned from Emma's father to address the reporters. She recognized his deeper, slower, press conference voice. "Emma Shea and I believed we were doing the right thing at the time." He reached for her hand, and she took it, moving away from her father to stand next to him.

"We made a mistake," Emma said.

"We're good people, and we like each other," Trent said. "We thought we could make a life together. Honestly, how many people have dreams of how marriage will be, only to find that it's not that way at all?"

"We wanted the dream," Emma said. "And we thought that if we had the perfect family and the great job and the pristine reputations, that happiness would come. But it didn't."

Trent nodded. "We realized pretty quickly how naive we'd been. Marriage doesn't suddenly make you compatible, it doesn't solve your problems. As a matter of fact, it creates more."

Emma's father barked at them. "If you make a vow, you see it through, come hell or high water. If it's a mistake, then you live with it."

"With respect, sir," Trent began, "we have been married one year, and we do not have any children. We see no reason to continue with something that is not working for either of us."

The reporter asked, "Some people might say that this is all an elaborate plan to cover up the fact that you are both adulterers. Were you in love with Abby when you married Emma Shea?"

"I'm sure some people will say that," Trent said, ignoring the last portion of the question.

"And what would you say to them?"

"Well, my first point should be obvious. It is none of their business."

"If you're running for the top political office in the state, those people might rightfully argue that your integrity is in question here. That it is, in fact, their business."

"Emma and I will be getting a divorce, and I don't know what the future holds, but I feel it is highly likely that if Mr. Willingham and Ms. Wingate agree, we will be dating them soon. But I cannot say this forcefully enough: we are not dating them now."

The entire crowd turned to Scruggs and Abby to answer the unspoken question: *Do you agree to date them?*

Abby answered first. "I am looking forward to exploring a relationship with Trent outside of our current friendship."

All eyes were then on Scruggs. He picked at his thumb, and Emma knew he'd rather be anywhere but there at that moment. "Emma is my dream girl," he said, his voice shaky. "She has been for a long time." His face turned bright red, and he hesitated before turning and leaving the room.

Emma wanted to go after him, but a reporter demanded her attention. "If you can't have Mr. Willingham, will you want your husband back?"

Emma shook her head. "I am prepared to be alone." She watched Scruggs walk out the front door. She didn't want to be alone, but what she'd said was true. She could be like Grandma Frannie and create a life for herself without a man.

That fact was nothing less than a revelation. Heck, she'd completed her college degree, worked as a nurse, and even managed to live by herself in an old beach house. She had a circle of friends, a grumpy cat, and successfully climbed a ladder to hang lights. Who had figured out how to get her car fixed? She had. Who was brave enough to leave a bad marriage? She was.

From a quiet corner, her expressionless mother came forward, and Emma braced herself for another attack. In a voice she barely recognized, her mother said, "My daughter will never be alone. She will always have her family." Then she slid an arm around Emma's waist. The warmth of her mother's body and the scent of her gardenia perfume was so very welcome.

"Mama," Emma exhaled, "you don't have to do this. I'm okay."

Both women's heads turned to Emma's father, who stood squeezing his hands into fists while his blood pressure shot so high that his face turned bright red.

"Yes, I do," she whispered. Then she addressed the crowd. "I'm gonna tell y'all a story. Have y'all ever heard of Firefly Girls? The old definition from the 1920s says they are unconventional women. They might do their hair different or behave outside of the rules of the day. Back then, it had something to do with drinking and smoking and dancing, but there is a new definition today, and it's a good one." She squeezed her daughter tightly into her side. "You see, my daughter is a Firefly Girl. She is unconventional in the way that she is ahead of her time. She is brave. She is kind. And she is a light, leading the way for others. Why should she stay with a man she doesn't love? Why would you try to shame her into it? He doesn't want to be married to her either! Let them both fly. Set them free."

Emma was moved to tears. Not only had her mother stood up for her, she'd heard her, she'd paid attention. "I can't believe it, Mama," she said. "I'll be right back." She left the room of people and jogged to the hall closet where she'd left a small bag of gifts.

She returned holding two jewelry boxes, each wrapped in gold paper and tied with a white ribbon. "Mama, this is for you." She turned to her friend. "And, Abby, this is for you."

As they opened the gifts, she explained. "When I was out looking for oyster shells the other day, I found these tiny olive shells, and they reminded me of the body of a firefly. Then I came across two sand dollars. You know how there are five doves of peace inside the shell? Well, I thought they kind of looked like firefly wings."

Abby had her box open and held the small seashell insect in the palm of her hand.

"And the inside of the oyster shell is reflective like the tail, so I put it all together and made these pins. We can make more whenever we want—every Firefly Girl should have one."

By the time Emma finished her explanation, Abby had the firefly pinned to the bodice on the right side of her dress. Her mother handed the gift to Emma to help pin it to her blouse. Without saying a word, both women stood with Emma in the middle and smiled for the cameras.

"Emma Shea," shouted a reporter. "You are an heiress. Why would you give such a cheap gift? Are those shells stuck together with hot glue?"

"I used a Weldbond glue," she said. "Hot glue wouldn't last." She cut her eyes to Trent, who looked away. She hoped he felt guilty about moving their money, about leaving her with so little.

"It's about the thought behind a gift, the meaning," her mother said with the voice of a reprimanding schoolmarm. "Not the price."

Her mother patted her on the arm. Emma couldn't wait to escape. What was done was done, what would be would be. She'd made her point, and there was nothing more she could do or say. The rest was up to God and the press.

"Do you need a ride home?" her mother asked once the attention was no longer focused on them.

"I think I do," she said.

Even though her plan hadn't gone horribly, aside from Scruggs disappearing, chances were that Christmas Day was either going to be a media disaster or a huge relief. She said goodbye to the guests she knew, hugged Trent and Abby, and didn't bother to address her father, who was clearly ignoring her.

"Are you going to leave Daddy here?" she asked her mother.

"That old goat can find his own ride home."

Emma must've looked surprised because her mother immediately added, "Now, don't you go getting your hopes up. I'm not leaving my marriage. That man might be worse than an old rooster pecking at me and everybody else the way he does, but I do love him. I really do." She smiled, and it wasn't the smile of an unhappy wife. "Now, let's get you back to Crickley."

Emma was ready. More than any place in the world, she wanted to be back in Crickley Creek.

Chapter Twenty-Two

EMMA AND HER mother had taken only one step down the front porch stairs before they noticed a person huddled on the freezing marble by the sidewalk. "You didn't leave!" Emma said, her heart about to explode at the sight of Scruggs.

He stood. "You really think I'd leave you?" He thrust his hands into his pants pockets. "We need to talk."

"Bye, Sugar." Emma's mother kissed her on the cheek and walked back into the house.

Scruggs's truck was as cold as the outdoors, and they were both quiet as the engine warmed up with the drive until the air finally blew warm. Emma broke the silence. "Thank you so much for coming. And for staying."

He took a minute before responding and she knew he was choosing his words carefully. "I felt like a pawn in there. I am being used in a game that I don't want to be a part of."

It made sense—and she hated that.

He drove toward the bridge. "I'm not going to do this again, Emma. It took me too long to let go of you." He took his eyes off the road long enough to appraise her. "I don't fit in that world, and I don't want to."

"I should've known that there would be questions about us dating after the divorce. We should've talked things through before I dragged you over there, and I never should have let them put you on the spot like that."

A small patch of black ice sent them skidding into a fish-tail before Scruggs gained control over the vehicle again. He slowed way down as they both caught their breath. "I'm not used to driving on ice," he said.

"You did great." She was still clutching the grab handle above the door. "That was scary."

They both concentrated on the street ahead before Emma broke the silence. She needed to get this next part over with. "Scruggs?"

"Mm-hmm."

"I…um. I need to tell you something. No one else knows this, and even though I'm always telling you I'm sorry, I really, really mean it."

He let out a large sigh and shook his head. "What?"

"There's a reason why I was confident about my plan tonight. See, back when I was living in that house I had to do something to get away from Trent. I felt like I was stuck, like I had no power. I knew I'd made a mistake by marrying him, and the pressure to be perfect, to be someone I wasn't, was too much."

"What are you saying, Emma?"

"The only way I saw to escape was to give those photos

to the press."

Scruggs was silent, staring at the road ahead for several seconds before he answered. "So, let me get this straight. You're the leak. You tipped off the press."

"Yes."

His nostrils flared as he absorbed her confession. "And you gave them pictures of me. Pictures of *us*, in order to launch yourself out of your marriage."

"Yes."

"And you never thought it'd be a good idea to talk to me about it first? To warn me that the girl who had ghosted me, the girl who wouldn't answer my phone calls, was about to make me look bad to thousands, or heck, maybe millions of people across the world? You didn't think you needed to at least warn me about that?"

It may have been motion sickness from riding in the truck, but Emma felt like she was about to heave.

"And you just did it again, didn't you? Just now. You've been talking to the press. You set this whole thing up, and you used me to get yourself out of a mess." His jaw was clenched as tightly as his hands on the steering wheel.

"No! That wasn't my plan at all! Not then, and not now." She turned her entire body to face him, praying he would understand. "I started trying to convince Trent to end the marriage on our honeymoon. I realized right away that we'd made a huge mistake. But I just got more and more desperate as the weeks passed by."

Scruggs's knuckles were white, his speed more than ten miles over the limit.

"I know you were in one of the pictures, but we weren't holding hands or acting like a couple. I mean, I expected them to speculate, but I never thought they would call you the other man or a home wrecker." The full weight of what she'd done hit her like buckshot to the face. He would never forgive her. How could he? She'd selfishly ruined his reputation for her own gain. This wasn't something they were in together, them against the media. She was the perpetrator and he was the innocent victim.

Scruggs looked straight ahead, his mouth in a thin line.

Emma tried to keep the emotion out of her voice. She couldn't appear like she was feeling sorry for herself or manipulating his feelings by crying. "I can see how bringing you there tonight felt the same way. Like an ambush."

"I didn't feel ambushed," he said, his voice deep and somber. "I felt like I let my heart get in the way of my good sense. Again."

The rest of the drive home was torture. Everything she thought to say sounded desperate or like an excuse. He was completely closed to her now. It was over. She had to accept that she would never again feel the privilege, the full-body tingle, and the sweet softness of his lips on hers. She watched his clench-jawed profile from the corner of her downturned eyes, and the longing, the desire for his love and acceptance, it all caused the volume inside of her head and heart to tick up a thousand decibels. She thought about begging him, anything to temper the loud voice telling her that she'll never see him again.

She monitored her breath and watched the passing homes, many of them with white lights outlining the house, spread across bushes, and wrapped around trees. The families inside were probably having a holiday ham or an oyster roast, whatever their tradition was. Kids might be unwrapping Christmas Eve jammies and putting out cookies for Santa. She liked to imagine the people in the twinkly homes loving each other, warm and cozy, laughing at the same old jokes, and not caring that a winter storm was hitting because there were presents under the tree and a day of togetherness ahead. Squeezing her eyes shut tight, she prayed. *Please don't let the media skewer Scruggs tomorrow. I'll take all the heat. Put it all on me. Please, God, protect him.*

An electric-yellow sign flashed in front of them. HAZARDOUS ROAD CONDITIONS. USE EXTREME CAUTION. Neither of them mentioned it. Their time for talking was over.

"Thanks again for coming," she said when he pulled into his driveway next door.

He said nothing.

She felt rooted to the spot, like if she didn't leave, they might come to an agreement. He might change his mind. He might not be gone from her forever.

But eventually, Emma had to force her body to move. As

stiff as a statue, her legs somehow moved from either sheer will or muscle memory. It was a miracle she didn't slip on the ice. She unlocked the frozen front door and jiggled the light switch several times until the foyer finally blinked into view. It was so dark outside that despite all of the windows, there was no ambient light at all. She pulled her jacket tight. Something had to be done to warm up the house or she was going to spend Christmas Eve as an icicle. She went to the kitchen for the box of matches she'd seen in a drawer, and from the windowed back door, she noticed an orange tail hanging off the blanket that covered the heating pad. She rushed over to see if Louie wanted to come inside, and the minute she opened the door, he popped up and ran onto the cold floor. He seemed surprised that the house was freezing, too. "Don't worry, Louie," she said. "I'm going to warm us up. I promise." It felt good to have the cat there, and she needed every scrap of comfort she could find.

He followed her into the family room where the old stove sat. She checked all around to make sure the flue on the pipe was open, remembering the YouTube video she'd watched when she first moved in. There was a stack of newspapers from 2015, and she scrunched them into tight balls and pressed them onto the bottom. Then she used the fatwood starters from an old metal drum nearby as kindling before stacking the logs on top.

Louie watched her work like he'd seen it all before, and that made her feel like she might be doing it right. The newspapers caught fire with only one match, and once the kindling ignited, she closed the door and locked it. Half expecting the room to fill with smoke, she was relieved when the only thing she felt was blissful, beautiful heat. She sat on the worn rug a few feet away, and Louie climbed into her lap. "We did it," she said, petting his head, grateful for the company. They sat that way, listening to the wood crack and burn as Louie's paws and Emma's toes slowly returned to normal body temperature.

Emma texted her mother. *"Thank you for what you did tonight."*

Then she texted Abby. *"Thank you so much for showing up."*

Neither person texted back, but that was okay. It was late. They were either still at the party or they'd gone to bed.

An hour's worth of reliving the ride with Scruggs passed, and Louie snored softly, but Emma's mind spun with too much to sort through, her heart too sick and remorseful to feel tired even though it was approaching midnight. Plus, she was about to host a party, she was up against her mother's deadline to move out, and she still had no idea where she was going to live after she left the little dilapidated home she'd grown to love.

But her immediate needs had to come first. She had to at least try to get some sleep, and even though the heat from downstairs would rise, she needed to get the space heater going in her bedroom. Louie barely moved as she carried him up the stairs and placed his sleepy body softly onto the middle of the bed, covering it with a blanket. "There you go, you little grump." When she leaned over and kissed his soft head, he stretched out a limb and spread his paw so wide that his claws fully extended before relaxing again into a cozy furry lump.

Emma changed into the warmest pajamas she had, then washed her face. The little heater was doing its job well, and by the time she came out of the bathroom, the room was almost comfortable. She walked past the big picture window on the way to bed and looked, as she always did, toward the moon and the sea. But there was more than just a moon outside, more than the infinite horizon of the dark midnight water. As a matter of fact, her view of those things was completely obscured by weightless white flakes of snow swirling and floating by the millions to the frozen ground.

It was Christmas, and it was snowing.

Snow was something Emma rarely saw. And snow in the Lowcountry? That was like an albino alligator—the white creatures existed, but you could easily go your whole life without ever seeing one. Emma grabbed her winter jacket and stuck her feet into the slippers, practically skiing down the stairs before throwing open the front door. At least an inch of snow covered everything, accumulating in the leaves of the overgrown plants and covering the street in icy whiteness. She wished she'd put on real shoes, but she ignored the cold and ran into the middle of the street for a long view of Blue Ghost Lane, each old building covered with white like icing on gingerbread houses.

Snow stuck to her hair and eyelashes, and she opened her mouth to taste it. A bank of clouds passed over and the full force and brightness of the moon was revealed. The yellow light reflected off the snow so brightly that it felt like daytime. A minute later, the streetlights turned off. Even the mechanical light sensors had been fooled. She laughed out loud and spun around, feeling a part of the magic, having no idea how it was possible to feel so thrilled when everything in her life was such a disaster. She picked up a handfuls of snow and threw them in the air, stopping when she saw him.

Scruggs had walked out onto Brownie's front lawn. "Can you believe it?" she yelled. "It's snow!"

He looked right at her, wearing a plaid bathrobe, probably Brownie's. She couldn't quite see the look on his face, so she waved at him. That was all it took. He turned around and went back inside the house. She was deflated, gutted. Again. And just like her, the streetlights realized they'd been stupid and blinked back on.

Her feet and fingers were freezing. She went inside and locked the front door. Then pulled a chair in front of the potbellied stove, took off her wet coat, and held her fingers and toes as close to the radiant heat as she could tolerate. Snow might be beautiful, but it would always be cold and wet. And when it was gone, they'd be left with a dirty, muddy mess.

Chapter Twenty-Three

I T WAS NOON on Christmas Day. There were no presents under the oyster shell Christmas tree, and no phone calls or texts of happy holiday wishes. Emma spent the morning avoiding social media and refusing to read any news. She had cooking to do. Her open house was from noon to five, and the menu would be assembled on her grandmother's red transferware and spread out on the bar of The Firefly Club. She'd already boiled the water, added cups of sugar and steeped the tea to serve cold in the large, hammered glass dispenser. She'd found boxes and boxes of glassware, and those were washed, the glasses and martini stems set on a large tray with a pitcher of pink peppermint cocktails for the guests who might like a more festive, and loaded, drink. Feeding people lunch and appetizers was much easier than dealing with a dinner meal—the expectations were lower.

The room upstairs was warm thanks to Brownie's little heater, and thanks to spruce candles in the center of each little table, it smelled like pine. It had been stressful and tenuous at times to pull a party together so quickly, but she managed to finish preparing all of the food with Louie at her feet eating bits of cheese and meat that she "accidentally" let fall to the ground. Bright light shone through every window from odd angles, intensely reflected from the snow that still covered the ground from the night before. She added logs to the stove, and it chugged out heat like it was the firebox of a steam locomotive and not a little black metal furnace in the corner.

Emma had been saving an off-white vintage lace flapper dress she'd found in her grandmother's closet for the occasion. It fit like it was custom-made for her. Her auburn hair was curled and clipped on one side with a sparkly barrette. People might think she was wearing a costume from the 1920s, but she didn't care. The party was her reward for setting things straight with Trent and the world, and it felt right to celebrate in one of her grandmother's dresses.

The only thing that wasn't ready to go was the crepe myrtle tree out front. The twinkle lights she'd worked so hard to wrap around it wouldn't turn on. She tried a new extension cord and checked the fuse box, but there was only so much she could do while wearing heels and a dress in twenty-eight-degree weather. Perfection was overrated anyway, and she didn't feel the need to live up to impossible expectations anymore. Brownie had told her to turn on the lights and she had. If they didn't stay on, she had no control over that.

Too anxious to sit, Emma wandered around the house like she had when she first arrived, inspecting all of the trinkets, opening drawers and cupboards. When she finally heard the sound of a car, she ran to the front window in time to watch it slowly drive past. It was past one o'clock. Maybe the frozen roads were keeping people away. She checked her phone. There was still not one text or phone call.

Louie was curled up on the floor by the stove, so she sat with him for a while. Had there been some terrible story in the press that was keeping people away? She was afraid to look. So she didn't. Instead, she went to the kitchen for the old black tray. *You have to take care of the roots before you can heal the tree.* She took her bag of homemade firefly pins that she'd wrapped for Christmas and stacked them artistically on the tray. She'd hoped to give one to Birdie and Krista and, eventually, Charlotte. They were Firefly Girls for sure, and she'd been so looking forward to giving them a pin and telling them what it meant. If Scruggs's mother showed up, she'd give her one, too.

By three o'clock, Emma had eaten a quarter of the artichoke dip, three cucumber sandwiches, and was buzzing from the caffeine and sugar of two large glasses of sweet tea. Her tray with the gifts was on a small table near the front of the hidden room, and her doorbell had not rung once. There were only two hours left of her open house, and she was pretty sure no one was coming. Not even Scruggs, whose truck was still parked next door.

Especially not Scruggs.

She rearranged the little gifts on the tray, balancing one

on the top of the triangle. *You have to take care of the roots.* She heard Brownie's voice in her head like it was her own, telling her what to do. "Fine," she said out loud. "I hear you, Brownie." If she wanted a relationship with her parents, which she did, someone had to behave differently. Someone had to break the cycle that they all repeated over and over again. The image of her mother explaining the Firefly Girls to the press the night before popped into her mind. Maybe that was a first step. Maybe one of them was willing to work with her, willing to change with her.

"Merry Christmas, Mama and Daddy," she texted.

Right away, her mother texted back, *"Merry Christmas, sweetheart."*

They were probably sitting in the all-white living room of their mansion on the golf course. Who knew if they even put up a Christmas tree. Did parents still do that when there wasn't a child around? It was the first Christmas she hadn't spent with them. The first Christmas that absolutely no one had given her a gift. Not that the gifts mattered. She was surprisingly unaffected by that part. What she cared about was that her family was celebrating without her.

Someone has to change. If I choose to keep them in my life, I have to take them as they are. And I have to stop seeking their approval. That's the only way to heal my roots.

She texted before she could change her mind. *"I have all kinds of food over here, and The Firefly Club is decorated for Christmas. I'd love for you both to come over."* She didn't mention that no one else had shown up. It was too humiliating to type out.

Her mother replied immediately. *"We've had wine. We can't drive."*

Well, that was that. She should've known. She'd put herself out there, only to be shot down. What else had she expected? Her roots were rotten. They were beyond healing. Her dad hadn't even bothered to respond. So there. She chose to have a relationship with them, but they didn't want one with her.

It made no sense, but she wanted to be mad at Brownie. *Believe it*, he'd said. "Believe what?" she practically screamed. "That no one likes me? That not one person cares? Is that it?" She kicked off her heels toward the open mirror door and nearly hit Louie as he peeked in. "Louie! I'm so sorry." She ran toward him, but he'd already made it to the bottom of the stairs. "I didn't mean to scare you!"

She plopped her rear onto the top step. What had Brownie said? She'd tried her best since his visit to remember every word, and she'd typed his advice into her phone for quick reference. First, he told her she wasn't ready to leave. *No kidding*, she thought, but she wasn't willing to get back together with Trent, and there was no way she would be getting engaged to Scruggs that very day, so she would soon have to find a place to stay until she found a job and do whatever it took to get Trent to give her money back. She felt her blood pressure rise. So, she sent him a text. Screw the fact that people were supposed to be nice on Christmas Day.

"Merry Christmas. If we're going to do this amicably, you need to put my money back into my account. Immediately." She put her phone back down on the wooden step a little too hard.

What else, Brownie? What other instruction of his would she fail to accomplish? She was in a fighting mood now.

His second instruction was to give something up in order to become her true self. Okay. Now, number two, that one she'd made some progress on. Somehow, in the past few weeks, not only had she lost her love for Louis Vuitton and transferred it to a cat, she'd left a life she'd built on a lie, and she'd recognized that she didn't have to live up to the perfection her parents required of her. She'd experienced firsthand how money couldn't buy love or happiness or peace or integrity. And, dammit, she was not put on this earth just to make a man look good.

"Was that the most important one, Brownie?" She spoke into the dark stairwell and listened as if there might actually be an answer. But the feeling in her stomach, the pride at her discoveries, and the knowledge that now that she knew better she would always do better, was enough. She still felt like fighting, but it had switched from *against* something to *for* something. She would fight for herself, not against anyone else. And, you know what? It was okay if no one showed up. There'd be another Christmas next year.

She scrolled up on her phone to read the rest of his advice. *Don't give up on my grandson.*

"Your grandson gave up on me," she said.

Turn on the lights.

"If you want me to turn on the lights, then you're going to have to send out an electrician."

On Christmas Day, believe it.

"I know Christmas isn't yet over, but Santa did not come down the chimney. My parents did not suddenly become decent people. And Scruggs did not decide to love me. So, Merry Christmas to me." She held up an imaginary glass for a clink, then slid down one stair and sat there for a second. Then she slid down another, and another, until she was all the way to the bottom. There was Louie, looking incensed that she'd taken so long.

He was next to the table that held an old Victrola in what resembled a small suitcase. Stacked underneath were record albums. Emma sorted through them until she found a Christmas album from the 1950s by Frank Sinatra. She lifted the needle and placed it gently onto the record. "Come on, Louie, let's dance. It's almost four o'clock, and no one is here but you and me. You want some fried chicken? Maybe a little taste of eggnog?" She spun him around, and his ears went back, his tail flipping madly just before he bit her hand—hard.

"Ow!" She dropped him and he, of course, landed on his feet before running to the back door. "Really?" she said, following him. "You bite the ham sandwich out of me when you're all I've got?"

Louie meowed loudly and aggressively.

"I set a box and some sand in the bathroom for you, you little bugger. There is no reason for you to freeze to death out there."

Louie hissed at her and scratched at the door.

"Fine," she said. He was outside before the door was completely open. "And don't bother coming back!" she yelled as the cat leapt away from her. "You're a jerk, anyway!"

The record was still spinning in the family room, and Frank Sinatra's voice filled the little house, instructing everyone that soon their troubles would be out of sight. "I've still got my troubles, Frank," Emma said out loud. She sat at the kitchen table listening to the words and staring at the porch door in case Louie came back. It was bright outside, and if it weren't for the snow, it would look like a warm day.

It only took opening the door for one second to know that it was still freezing. If Louie didn't come back in ten minutes, she would put on something warm and go find him. Frank Sinatra still crooned in the next room about faithful friends and merry little Christmases. The nostalgia the song created, her worry for Louie, and her disappointment over the failed party felt like she was on the edge of an emotional cliff—like one swift wind might knock her down so far that she could never climb back up.

Emma jumped when her doorbell rang. She looked at

the time: four thirty. Her party shoes were upstairs and she had orange fur all over the front of her dress, but someone was at her door! She ran to answer it.

"Something's wrong with your tree lights," Birdie said, frowning at the dim, flickering lights on the crepe myrtle. "I believe you might have an electrical issue." She forced a huge wrapped package into Emma's arms. "Here's a little gift for you. It's an air fryer. I got two of them."

"Thank you, Birdie."

The woman was already inside and heading toward the kitchen. Her extra-tall husband stopped at the door and bent to give Emma a kiss on the cheek. "Merry Christmas, Miss Emma," he said before handing her a plate full of Christmas cookies.

"Merry Christmas, Ashby."

"Sorry we're early," he said. "Birdie's been chomping at the bit all day."

Early? "No problem at all," Emma said, wondering if everyone was under the impression that the party started instead of ended at five. Her whole body tingled with relief. "I'll be right back," she said. "I left my shoes upstairs."

She took the stairs two at a time, a burst of happy energy taking over. She quickly fixed her makeup, wiped the orange fur from her dress, and stuffed her feet into her heels. Frank Sinatra crooned about mistletoe and holly downstairs, and Emma could barely contain her happiness.

"There's a cat at your door!" Birdie yelled.

Thank God. "Can you please let him in?" Emma yelled back, running as quickly as she could in heels. Louie was sauntering around the kitchen as if he hadn't just been very naughty and at risk of freezing. "I'm so sorry," she said to him while offering several cat treats and petting him while he ate. "I'm glad you're back."

"I will never understand single people's fascination with cats," Birdie said.

Louie led the way upstairs and, although Birdie's painted-on eyebrows held a perpetual look of surprise, for once, the rest of her matched. "Oh my word," she said. "My word!" She stepped down into the room and walked from spot to spot like a pinball before scurrying back to her husband and grabbing his arm. "Can you believe it? It's a genuine speakeasy! It's the real deal!"

Ashby was a reticent man, but his face said it all—it was twice as long and thin with his mouth hanging open.

The doorbell rang again, and Emma practically skipped downstairs. "Hey! Merry Christmas!" Krista said. She and Johnny were dressed in matching plaid button-downs, only Krista wore hers as a belted dress with boots. She handed Emma a hostess gift and a platter of chips and dip. "Your lights on that tree are so pretty."

Emma stuck her head outside. The lights were still blinking, but much stronger this time, they weren't as subtle and weak. "Thank you. I'm so glad you're here! The party is upstairs. Help yourself to food and drink!"

There was a car pulling up as she said it, so Emma stayed at the door. It was a tricked-out Porsche, and she knew exactly who was inside.

Chapter Twenty-Four

TRENT PARKED IN front of the house and opened the door for Abby. He was in his usual slim suit, and she climbed out wearing sequined pants the same red color as the flowers she held. Not everyone could pull off a pair of pants like that, but Abby was confident enough to do it. The sight of the two of them reassured Emma that she'd done the right thing. There was something about them that simply went together like cookies and milk, or more appropriately, bourbon and cream.

"I hope we got the time right," Abby yelled from the street before she jogged carefully to the front door. "I thought it was earlier, but your mother said it was at five." She handed Emma the flowers.

Her mother? "You are right on time," Emma said, hugging her. "Thank you for the flowers."

"Hey, there, hubby," she teased Trent. "Nice of you guys to come."

"There is a lot to celebrate," Trent said with his old smile back as he guided Abby into the house.

Emma wondered what he meant by that, but she blew it

off as she led them up the stairs to the party, still astounded that people had showed up. She mentally went through her guest list. Of course, Charlotte and Will wouldn't be coming. Most likely, they had just gotten the baby home from the hospital. Her parents weren't coming, so that left Scruggs and his family. She'd invited them, but after the Nikki fiasco and considering Scruggs wouldn't even deign to talk to her during a rare weather event in the middle of the night, everyone who was coming was probably already here. Which was fine. A small party was better than no party at all.

She stopped at the door to the secret room, watching her friends sip peppermint martinis at the various high-top tables near the bar. Most of them had a plate of food in front of them and talked to each other like they were enjoying the togetherness that Christmas was supposed to bring. Frank Sinatra's singing wafted up the staircase like it was a sound tunnel, and soon Birdie was singing along to "Jingle Bells" in between bites of cheese and salami. Emma put the flowers next to the oyster tree with the previous gifts and stepped back to take in the scene. The room came alive with the people.

Now, why did her mother tell everyone to come at five? Was she trying to sabotage her own daughter? Emma walked over to the table where Birdie was holding court with Krista and Johnny. "Can I ask y'all a question?" Emma began. "Did my mother tell you what time this party started?"

"Now, now, don't get mad at her," Birdie said. "She

came into the coffee shop the other day and we got to talking."

"Hold on." Emma put up her hand in a stop motion before placing it on her forehead. "My mother was at Tea and Tennyson?"

"Well, yes. She was meeting a man there."

"What?" Emma felt faint.

"Not like that!" Birdie said. "It looked to be a professional meeting."

"When?"

"Oh, I don't know. When was that, Krista?"

"I wasn't there," she said. "I have no idea."

"Shoot. My days run together sometimes. I believe it was the day the newspaper called you a gold digger. That was only a couple of days after they called your husband a cheater. When was that? A couple of mornings ago? Anyhoo, now that y'all have been vindicated, I guess it doesn't matter."

Vindicated? What was she talking about?

"I told her about your invitation, and I might have mentioned that evening parties were much more fun. I didn't understand why you'd have something at the lunch hour on Christmas Day. Everybody knows that noon is for falling asleep on the couch after getting up early to open gifts and eating too many cinnamon rolls." Birdie took a large swig of her martini. "Your mama agreed with me, so we decided."

Emma laughed. "So, you and my mother decided my

party should be later, but no one thought to tell me?"

Birdie gasped. "Did she not tell you? I mean, we told everybody else. All of the Crickley Creek folks, anyway."

"Did you tell Scruggs?"

"Oh yes. I told him this morning when I called to wish him a Merry Christmas. I said, *I will see you at Emma's house tonight at five o'clock*, and I told him to have his mama bring her banana pudding. See, she crunches up the Nilla Wafers and mixes them with pecans, brown sugar, and, I think, butter. Yes, it's got to be butter. Then she spreads it all over the top—"

"So, Scruggs and his family are coming?" Emma interrupted, feeling like she'd just crested the peak of a roller coaster and was about to speed straight into the ground.

"Well, I believe so, yes."

Trent came over and put his arm around her. "This place is really cool," he said.

Emma introduced him and Abby to everyone at the table. "Let's make a toast!" Birdie held the last sip of her drink in the air. "To making mistakes!"

Emma wasn't holding a glass, so she "air clinked" with Trent.

"To making mistakes!" Trent and Abby said with enthusiasm.

Emma had to get to the bottom of the toast and the vindication comment, but the doorbell had just sent her heart rate back up to the top of the roller coaster. She nearly twisted an ankle scurrying down the stairs to the door, wondering if Scruggs was on the other side.

There, looking like a judgmental pucker was frozen on her face, stood Virginia Buchanan. Emma hadn't even invited her. She barely knew the woman aside from all the talk about her being Charlotte's wicked stepmother and the haughtiest, craziest blue blood around. "Welcome," Emma said, opening the door wide.

"Merry Christmas," Virginia said flatly, handing her a small bag from a boutique in Charleston. "I have brought you a candle. It is made from beeswax and essential oils. Only the finest, of course." She made no attempt to hide the fact that she was appraising everything in sight. "This house is not at all what I expected."

"Thank you," Emma said, taking the bag. "It has been in my family for generations."

Virginia paused, no doubt considering clarifying that she did not mean it as a compliment. "Do I hear the guests upstairs?"

"You sure do. The Firefly Club is straight up the stairs to the right."

There were cars busily parallel parking all along the street in front of her house. Who were they? The lights on her crepe myrtle shone such a bright steady glow that she could almost see inside their windows but not quite. The lights from next door helped, too. Not only were the porch lights on, but the entire front of the house was aglow. And

Scruggs's truck was still in the driveway.

She stood in the doorway, ready to welcome her guests, whoever they were. As they approached the house, she began to recognize them. They were Junior Leaguers and storytime moms, divorcees and widows and teachers. They were all regulars at Tea and Tennyson, and she knew them from when she used to work there. Birdie stood behind her at the door with her phone set to record.

"They all saw your mama talking about y'all's new girl group on the television," she said. "Welcome to the club, Firefly Girls!" she exclaimed. "Smart of y'all to carpool. Hey, there, Bernadette! Did you remember to bring the Sweet Tea Vodka?" Birdie leaned over to whisper in Emma's ear, "She works at the Firefly distillery. Doesn't it fit with our theme so nicely?" Birdie ushered in woman after woman, pointing them and their food offerings upstairs.

When Emma looked out the door again, a group of people were making their way from Brownie's house next door. They were coming! She looked from face to face for Scruggs. There was his mother, his stepfather, his auntie Janelle, and gosh darn it, the girl in the leather pants behind them was Nikki. Nikki was not supposed to be invited, but that was the least of her worries.

There was no Scruggs. His family was coming without him. Was it a ploy to smooth things over and cover for the fact that their son would never speak to her again? She was genuinely happy to see them, but the message they were sending by showing up without Scruggs was the proverbial nail in the coffin for her relationship with him. It was truly dead. It was over.

"Welcome!" she said as brightly as she could. "I'm so glad you're here!"

"Where's Scruggs?" Birdie asked.

His mother answered carefully, "Marshall is exhausted from a long day. I don't think he's coming." She smiled apologetically at Emma.

Nikki handed her a clear-topped box filled with pastel-colored macarons. "Merry Christmas," she said, her red lips no longer in a tight line. "They're coconut."

"Ooooh!" Birdie said. "I love me some coconut macarons."

The significance wasn't lost on Emma. It was possible that they, along with her presence, were Nikki's version of an apology. Most unexpected. "Thank you, Nikki. They look delicious."

"I'm told they are," she said, making her way up the stairs.

When they finally closed the front door, Birdie turned the phone on herself. "Come here, Emma," she said, pulling her in close for a video selfie. "We are the O-G Firefly Girls, right? At least for this decade. Women on the internet, hear me now," Birdie declared. "If you are ahead of your time, if you are changing the world with your love and positivity, if you are a good person, a kind person, a strong person, and not one of those selfish, *everything is about me, tailgate a person all the way to the Piggly Wiggly, and then steal the good parking space* kind of person, then you, too, are a member of our auspicious club." She squeezed Emma's cheek into her own. Her breath smelled like peppermint and alcohol. "Now, wave bye-bye to my fans!"

Emma obediently smiled and waved.

"Good," Birdie said after she turned off the camera. "Now that I have done my job as an influencer, I am expected upstairs in the club."

"I'll be right there," Emma said. Now that there was a crowd, she needed to move the old Victrola upstairs so people could hear it better.

Another car had arrived, so Emma quickly scuttled the music up the stairs and ran back down. It was amazing to her how many people had included her in their plans for Christmas Day. Weren't they all supposed to be eating with their huge families at long tables somewhere thanking God for Jesus, for the food, and for each other?

She squinted as a couple walked hand in hand up the street to her house. Since a man was in tow, it probably wasn't one of Birdie's coffee shop posse.

No, it wasn't one of them at all.

It was her parents.

She didn't know whether to run toward them or away from them, so she stayed leaning against the doorframe for support. Since when did they hold hands? Hopefully, they weren't here to kick her out. Every now and then they would use the "united front" parenting technique. She hated that. It just meant that they were ganging up on her.

And yes, technically, she was supposed to be gone by Christmas Day. And yes, instead of leaving, she was having a party. But her suitcase was mostly packed, and she had plans to get her car from the shop the next day. She was only one day late, and it'd been snowing! Plus, she had no money, thanks to Trent, and she didn't want to leave the cat outside when it was so cold, and her life had been so danged stressful lately, and the house really needed someone to live in it, to take care of it. She barely saw them approach as she racked her brain for more excuses. Before she knew it they were standing in front of her. She opened her mouth to say hello, then closed it again. Her mother was dressed as a flapper in a gold dress with fringe, and her father wore a cream dinner jacket and two-toned shoes.

"We weren't really drunk on wine," her mother said. "We just wanted to surprise you."

She didn't realize how much she'd missed their love and approval until they were in front of her, looking like they used to when she was little. Like they weren't angry or disappointed. She wanted to throw herself into her daddy's arms, but she held back.

She noticed her mother was wearing the seashell firefly pin.

"This is for you," her mother said, handing her an envelope decorated with angels blowing trumpets and twinkling yellow stars.

"Thank you," Emma said. "I'm so sorry that I don't have a gift for you this year."

"That article they published today was gift enough," her dad said.

"What article?"

Her parents looked at each other like they couldn't believe she'd just asked that question. "The one on the front page of the *Courier*?" her mother said. "The one with the headline, ARE MISTAKES ALLOWED?"

Her dad actually smiled. He *smiled*. "The abridged version is this." He spoke like a professor. "Generally, constituents do not allow mistakes to be made in politics. But do they allow mistakes in a candidate's personal life? Sometimes. They used Trent's Christmas Eve party as the best example of truth-telling, of coming clean, and of behaving like adults. Now, that is not to say that there isn't a world of people out there upset that you're giving up on the marriage, and are actively looking for more dirty secrets. But Trent's advisors believe that as long as you two remain friendly, like you were at the party, the split may even work to his advantage."

"Are you okay with this, Daddy?" Emma was relieved about the article, but she knew about the evolution of stories, and how one loud voice that told a lie over and over again could create an untrue "truth." She didn't want to get too excited.

His face darkened. "It hurts me worse than you will ever know that you won't be first lady. We raised you to be something special." It was subtle, but her mother squeezed the knuckles of his hand together aggressively. "But, you're my daughter, Emma Shea, and I don't want you to spend your life unhappy."

Emma's gaze met her mother's. *Is this true?*

Mrs. Abernathy shrugged and smiled, then walked to the empty table where the record player had been and flipped through the albums underneath, pulling out Count Basie and Duke Ellington. Then she carried the albums up the stairs like she owned the place, which she did.

"We'll start here," she said when they got to the bar where Emma had put the phonograph on the corner. Clarissa removed Frank Sinatra's Jolly Christmas from the turntable and replaced it with the piano, trumpets, saxophones, trombones, and an entire rhythm section of the Count Basie orchestra. "That ought to get the dancing started," she said before shimmying into the crowd to the beat of the music. Emma's father followed, his eyes as big as headlights as he took everything in.

She thought her parents only danced at weddings. Those two were full of surprises.

Chapter Twenty-Five

BIRDIE SHOOED THE guests out by eleven, making sure that each one took home the leftovers of what they brought. "Wash your own dish," she told the lady who wanted to leave the rest of the cold BBQ meatballs for Emma. After the crazy emotional swings of the day, Emma felt a hundred years old and was grateful for the help. She had a lot to do the following day between cleaning, packing, picking up her car, and finding a cheap hotel. Plus, despite the revival of The Firefly Club, the fun and bonding, the good food, laughter and dancing, she'd spent the whole night with one ear toward the front door. Would Scruggs come by? She'd sneak peeks out her downstairs window to his house, which remained brightly lit. Was he okay? Was he awake?

Alone again in the house with only Louie for companionship, she picked up used napkins and stacked dirty plates. But her mind was stuck on Scruggs.

I won't call you.

I won't knock on your door.

I won't smile and wave when I see you.

I won't ask about you or look you up on the internet.

I won't make shepherd's pie and think about how it's your favorite dish.

I won't look for you every time I drive by Tea and Tennyson, or order a coffee drink, or see Legos or flowers or little brown dogs.

I won't wonder if you're thinking about me.

Her thoughts became a pledge both to him and to herself.

I won't text you on your birthday, or to check if you're sick or hurt. You'll become a shadow in my past—a could-have-been, a should-have-been.

I promise you, though, with all of my heart, I won't forget you. I'll never completely let go.

There was less than an hour left of Christmas. It took several trips to carry all of the used glasses and dishes into the kitchen. She stood barefoot at the sink and rinsed each one, stacking them on the counter with plans to hand wash them with soap in the morning. It was closing in on midnight, and she was exhausted. The wood in the old stove had long ago turned to ash, and Louie had been snoring on the bed upstairs for the better part of an hour. She dried her hands and pulled the barrette from her hair, rubbing at the sore spot it left on her scalp. It was time to cozy up in the warmest room in the house and get some sleep.

"Emma?"

She spun around toward the back door.

Scruggs stood at the glass, softly knocking.

She wasn't sure she should open it. She'd just pledged to leave him alone. "Come in," she said instead. "It's cold out there."

"I'm sorry I missed the party."

He was? "It's okay. I understand."

He stayed near the door, even though she had walked farther into the kitchen. She doubled back. Clearly, his visit was going to be a short one.

"I might be crazy," he said. "But do you remember when I told you how my granddaddy would use my grandmother's baking flour to leave Santa's footprints from the fireplace to the tree?"

She nodded. The poor boy had believed in Santa until middle school because of those footprints.

"I think I'm losing my mind." He pointed behind him.

She stuck her head out, and to her amazement, there were clear boot prints making a path directly to her back door and a second set made from tennis shoes that led straight to where Scruggs stood.

"I swear, I didn't do it. Look," he said, placing his much bigger foot on the other print.

"They just showed up out of nowhere," he said. "I was, uh, working on something my mama brought over, and when I glanced outside, there they were."

"Maybe your stepdad walked over here before they left?"

"I don't think so." He finally stepped inside, and she shut the door to keep the warm air in.

LAURIE BEACH

If Brownie hadn't personally visited her, she wouldn't have believed it. But there it was, still Christmas Day, and Brownie had left footprints for his grandson like he always had before. Only instead of leading from the fireplace to the tree, they led straight to Emma.

"I think my granddaddy is trying to tell me something," Scruggs said.

She remembered Brownie's words, whispering them more to herself than to him, "Believe it."

"I do," he said.

"What do you think it means?" she asked.

"Hold on," he said. "I need to go get something." Throwing open the back door, he took one step out and stopped. She heard him mumble something in disbelief. "Emma, come here."

She stepped onto her back porch with him.

"The boot footprints are gone."

Sure enough, the only prints left in the snow were made by Scruggs's old worn-out Vans. She gasped. "It really is true."

He seemed to be in deep thought.

"Why?" she asked.

"I know why," he said. "Be right back." He jogged next door and returned less than a minute later holding something behind his back.

"What do you have?"

"Something for you." There, in a vase, were her Lego

230

flowers, reassembled, each piece clicked back together, beautiful and whole again. "My mama noticed them on your table and brought them to me to fix."

Emma couldn't believe how many good things were happening. Even down to the smallest detail, like the silly little plastic flowers that she loved so much were whole again. "Thank you." She smelled them and then felt ridiculous for sniffing plastic. She laughed nervously.

"I know you, Emma. See, that's the problem. I know you like to watch movies in the closet because you think big rooms are scary. I know you hate parallel parking, and you'd walk a mile instead of trying. I know that hummingbirds scare you, but you'd let a pelican take a fish straight from your hand. And I know you have a raised mole on your right shoulder—I told myself I'd make sure you get it checked every year."

He stared ahead like there was a canyon coming up and he was resigned to drive off of it. "That article, are mistakes allowed? Yes. They have to be. See, I know you are a kind person; I know you're not a liar and that you try not to hurt people. I also know that you're not perfect."

She stayed silent. Holding strands of her hair between her fingers, she rubbed them together for comfort. Was it possible that he could forgive her?

"I've been hurt, and I've been mad as hell. But here's the thing: I think my granddaddy is telling me not to cut the line," he said. "I think he's telling me to fight for you."

"Like Frannie did for him long ago," Emma whispered, her heart leaping.

"Maybe she's up there helping." He shrugged. "I can't make sense of it, so I guess I'll just…"

"Believe it," Emma filled in.

"Yes." Scruggs smiled. It was open and pure, like she'd never betrayed him or broken his heart. "You know," he said, "when you first moved in, Granddaddy said there was a girl next door who was perfect for me." He turned to her, taking both of her hands, his voice gruff with emotion. "Of course it was you."

Was this really happening? Had Brownie really led him to her again? He looked back out at the ocean, and she followed suit, amazed by Brownie's gift and the vast sea of unseen, undiscovered life. The passing storm had swept away the clouds, and a sky full of stars shone like Christmas twinkle lights, like the lighted tails of fireflies, and like the sparks of a true love imbued with the power to outshine mistakes.

A light that burned brighter than time itself.

He squeezed her hands, and she looked up at him, her heart racing. His face was mere inches away. She recognized the old intensity, and when his lips touched hers, it was like a rip tide taking her out to sea—impossible to fight the feelings as they overtook her. Their mouths communicated the desperation they both felt. How had they waited so long? How had they survived without each other? Thank God it wasn't too late.

The pressure of their kisses increased as their breaths shortened and the need for each other intensified. Their bodies pressed together so no chill could come between them. No man, no expectations, no family, nothing in the world could ever come between them again.

She didn't just believe it, she knew it.

Epilogue

THE WOOLLY BEAR caterpillar was right. He was almost all black when Emma found him on the rim of the pot out front, the rust-colored band on his midsection less than a quarter of an inch wide. And, sure enough, the winter that year had been severe. Woolly bears didn't lie.

Emma Shea Broadway was now Emma Shea Abernathy once again, but to the people of Crickley Creek, she was simply Emma. She made her home at 19 Blue Ghost Lane, thanks to a generous gift her mother tucked into a card on Christmas Day. The arrangements had been made with a lawyer at Tea and Tennyson just two days before the party. The house was not part of her now-empty trust—it was a gift from Emma's mother and grandmothers to be given when the time was right.

And, if you asked Louie, the time was definitely right. He had finally chosen a house in which to belong, a person to love, and a visiting dog named after a breakfast food to tolerate. He clearly had plans to spend his senior years in a warm place with fresh bowls of food and water, and a human who let him sleep on the bed. He used the new cat door that

Scruggs installed in Emma's kitchen to come and go as he pleased. That way he could continue his daytime job of harassing unsuspecting beachgoers.

It took only one meeting with lawyers to disentangle Emma's finances from Trent's, and with her new job at the hospital in Charleston and her home paid for, Emma had enough extra income to commission little gold firefly pins for the Firefly Girls and her one special Firefly Guy. What had started with once a month social meetings upstairs in the speakeasy turned in to a group of women who supported not only each other but the community at large. It didn't take long to realize that as a group they could help more than they could as individuals. Birdie was great at figuring out who was in need, and Krista used her skills to figure out what sort of help was necessary and how to get it to them. They were a regular little charity group.

Charlotte always showed up with Charlie, who usually napped or sat like a little blob in his car seat. But with each passing month, he achieved more milestones and was now sporting two bottom teeth and a smile that made the whole room smile back. He was even growing into his ears. Much to everyone's surprise, Virginia never missed a meeting. She and Scruggs's mother had become good friends. As a matter of fact, they'd become friends with Emma's mother, too. Maybe money attracted money. Of course, Birdie made sure she was included in all of their get-togethers and made it her personal mission to keep them humble.

The next group outing was to the marsh for Krista's and Johnny's wedding. The Firefly Girls would all be there—all twenty of them. And that number was growing fast thanks to Birdie's latest viral video entitled Women Without Manners. It was all about the Firefly Girls and how sometimes, in order to be ahead of your time, in order to fight the evils of the world, and in order to help others, one must forget all manners and simply get things done. The message resonated all the way to California, where a woman reached out to Birdie to find out how to start a group of her own.

Brownie's headstone was delivered on a warm spring afternoon, and Scruggs took Emma to the Crickley Creek Memorial Gardens to see it. His plot lay next to his wife's inside a short black iron fence under the shade of two Spanish moss-covered live oaks. Both large stones were cut into the ground, per his wife's request. She'd wanted future generations to picnic there, to be comfortable, so Brownie had added two small concrete benches on either side. Her stone simply read MARY ELIZABETH HOWELL and his BROWN ODGERS HOWELL with one small epitaph at the bottom: TOGETHER IN DEATH, AS IN LIFE.

"I'm happy for him," Scruggs said, letting go of her hand in order to brush dirt and grass from one corner.

"Me too." Emma placed a dozen daisies in between the two slabs. Then she kissed her fingertips and placed them on the cool carving of his name. "Thank you, Brownie. Thank you for the good advice, and thank you for leading Scruggs to me. Please tell Grandma Frannie that I'm healing my roots, and that her house has helped."

There was a party for the opening of the day spa at Tea and Tennyson that night, and Emma needed to get back to her little green house on the beach to get ready. She took Scruggs's hand in hers and they walked in silence among the gravestones to where his truck was parked. For Emma, it was a reflective silence despite the loud chirping of the songbirds and the distant roar of a lawnmower. She wanted to remember every detail about the man who had known her grandmothers and who had helped her so much—each crinkle around his eyes, the way he parted his thick white hair, the old leather belt he always wore to hold up his too-big pants, the crepey skin on his thick hands, and the sound of his laughter. The man who had opened the door to her past, and led the way for her future. She would always be grateful for Brownie.

The sky was blue, and the weather back to the usual Lowcountry warm. Scruggs rolled down a window for fresh air on the ride home. "You know what question my grand-daddy always used to ask? He'd say, *Who do you want to be?*" He deepened his voice to imitate Brownie. "He was ornery, he wouldn't even wait for an answer. He'd just say, *then be it.*"

"That sounds like him," Emma said. "He never asked me that question, but I've had to think about it a lot in the past two years."

"I think you landed on the right answer."

She turned to face him as he drove. "What do you think the answer is?"

"Let me see." He chuckled, taking sideways glances at her. "Who does Emma want to be? Oh, I know. Emma wants to be a collector of Lego gifts."

Playfully, she smacked his arm. "The flowers are enough, thank you very much."

"Emma wants to be—no, she is desperate to be the wife of an architect."

"Not yet, Mister Man. Call off the caterers. We're just getting started."

"Damn," he said, pretending to be upset. "Okay, that's coming later. Let's see. Emma wants to be—"

"I'll tell you," she interrupted. "Emma wants to be just as she is. A good person, not a perfect person. A girl who's in love with a strange-named guy, living in a magical house, trying to make the world a better place." She made a face. "That sounds so trite and cliché."

"Not if it's the truth."

As they pulled onto Blue Ghost Lane, Emma noticed that the lights on her crepe myrtle out front were shining as steady and bright as nighttime stars. "I don't think they're plugged in," she said, specifically remembering that she'd unplugged them weeks prior. She'd made the decision to turn them on only when she had friends coming to The Firefly Club, just like her great-great-grandmother had. And then only at night. She had to pay the electric bill now, and there was no use wasting money.

They both exchanged a look of wonder. "Do you think—?" Emma began.

He pulled into her driveway, threw the truck into Park, then ran to where the extension cord lay on the ground next to the outlet. Standing next to the glowing lights, he held up the unplugged end and laughed like he'd discovered the Holy Grail. Such things actually existed. It was proof that there was more to life than could be seen.

"I guess we'll just have twinkle lights year-round," he said, shrugging.

"I'm okay with that," Emma laughed. "It'll be like Christmas every day."

The End

Acknowledgements

Many thanks to the experts at Tule Publishing for the existence of this book, especially Jane Porter, who gave me a chance, Julie Sturgeon, who is an expert at making stories better, and Nan Reinhardt who catches all of my comma mistakes. Also, Meghan Farrell, Mia Gleason, and Cyndi Parent for keeping the Tule engine running so well.

Susie Barton will always have my heart for paving the way for my career. Diana Kalliaras is my travel buddy and just the kind of deep thinker and detail-noticer that I need. Sue Backer is my original friend-turned-editor and if it wasn't for her support, I may never have kept going with this whole writing thing. Dawn Lee Schaeperkoetter and Edi McNinch are my beta readers extraordinaire and experts on the Lowcountry, plus delightful people. My fabulous Street Team has my back so well that I get giddy just thinking about them. And I can't forget the Battisfore family, Pamela and Kiki LeBaron, Juls Lopezi, Kelly Hall, Michelle Myers, Suzie McCormac, Krista Roodzant, Sharon Allen, and so many other supportive friends who I feel extraordinarily lucky to have in my life.

My stepson and daughter-in-law, Drew Bixler and Emily

Beers, are great encouragers and deserve tons of appreciation. My daughters, Allison, Natalie, and Brooke have taught me what it's like to have a fan club, and they keep me feeling like I actually have a talent worth sharing. Love and thanks to my beloved family: Bill and Maureen Lokken, Sharon Reese, Chris and Susie Herring, Clarissa Herring, Charlie and Meggan Lokken Bishop, Ken and Holly Wenzl, Ron and Noelle Noggle, Alice and Nick Perrins, Millie and Michael Steber, and all of my fabulous nieces and nephews.

Most of all, every bit of gratitude imaginable to my husband, Bryan Reese. He makes my dreams come true.

If you enjoyed *Christmas in Crickley Creek,*
you'll love the next book in the…

Crickley Creek series

Book 1: *The Firefly Jar*

Book 2: *Blink Twice If You Love Me*

Book 3: *Christmas in Crickley Creek*

Available now at your favorite online retailer!

About the Author

Photographer: Stephanie Lynn Co

Laurie Beach is a former news reporter, advertising producer, and political press secretary who, after raising four children, is parlaying her love of reading and writing into a career as an author. She is a sucker for elderly people, grumpy animals, and happy endings. Having grown up in Alabama, she loves novels set in the South. Laurie now lives in California with her husband and their spoiled old dog.

Thank you for reading

Christmas in Crickley Creek

If you enjoyed this book, you can find more from all our great authors at TulePublishing.com, or from your favorite online retailer.

TULE
PUBLISHING

Made in United States
Troutdale, OR
12/11/2024